To A

Our favorite critic

Is a war ever over?

Enjoy

Ray + Jewell

The Soul of Private McFarron

AKA
Nate Tolar

Nate Tolar

Chapter One

A sudden hush fell over the raucous noise of the jungle as the short, muscular figure in forest green battle dress cautiously stepped out of the dense foliage and stopped, his rifle held at the ready across the front of his body. The blue steel bayonet affixed to the end of the barrel glinted ominously in the mid-day sun as he stood motionless, his Asian features inscrutable while his head moved with a slow deliberation, assessing the wide glade. His dark menacing eyes studied the surrounding pungent growth and the graveled streambed yawning before him, dry now in the summer heat and relentless sun.

When he was satisfied there were no sounds or signs of a presence or recent passage in the loose gravel or the imposing vegetation ahead, he raised the rifle slowly and motioned forward.

He then turned to his right and stepped backward several paces as two more swarthy figures, also in forest green battle dress, cautiously emerged from the jungle. They carried identical rifles with bayonets affixed, and separated to take a stance across from each other where they had just emerged from the concealing growth.

All three men held their rifles at the ready position as the column of eight gaunt prisoners in tattered remnants of their U.S. Army camouflage fatigues made their way into the open.

Their hands were tightly secured in front of them with barbed wire, and in the absence of any kind of head covering, the prisoners squinted at the harshness of the sun as they staggered from the shading foliage and slowly made their way across the weeded expanse to the streambed.

Each of the eight prisoners, in turn, carefully made their way down the shallow, crumbling shoal, trudged across the sand and loose gravel to grope their way up the far bank. Several additional guards had stepped from the jungle and were marshalling them into a group, a holding line, until they had all crossed the streambed.

While the column of haggard prisoners carefully negotiated the coarse, uneven terrain and the loose footing of the dry streambed, the ninth prisoner, a blond young man, laboriously emerged from the jungle, dragging his left leg. Two additional guards were prodding him insolently along, his hands bloody from the tightness of the barbed wire restraining them and the need to heave his arms upward for momentum to drag the useless leg into position with each step.

Private Jamie McFarron stopped just clear of the jungle growth, grimacing as he drew in a slow guarded breath. The sight of the other prisoners arduously making their way across the harsh terrain made his own situation appear even more hopeless.

His head fell forward with a consuming weariness as he stood there, his chin on his chest at the sight of the ordeal ahead. His leg had surely become infected by the bamboo stake in the shallow pit that had penetrated his calf the night he was captured.

The leg was swollen to twice its normal size now, and without any feeling other than an internal burning sensation, but he refused to mention it for fear that they might abandon him here in the jungle. Or at least remove his shoe to examine his leg, the shoe he had hidden a dog tag in.

And then the second day out of camp, or was it the third, he had lost all sense of time and the basics of humanity. This morning the belligerent guard had given him a vicious jolt to the ribs with a rifle butt for failing to raise his bound hands and wait for permission to speak before he feverishly asked for a drink of water.

Jamie, standing quietly there in the blinding sun despite the guard's incessant ranting, suddenly threw his head back with a muted whimper at the sudden jolt of the guard's rifle butt to his kidney. He swayed with the punch, barely managing to keep his balance, but made no effort to move forward even though he was well aware of the penalty for disobedience.

That morning at first light, as they were breaking camp, one of the guards had kicked Jamie's swollen foot and motioned for him to get up from where he had spent the night on the moist humus of the jungle floor. With his left leg useless and the rest of his body stiff from the cold wetness of the night rain, all he could manage to do was raise himself onto his other knee and his bound hands, but with nothing to pull up to, he had settled back onto his one heel and began to move his head slowly from side to side in resignation.

Rebel, the self-appointed leader of their little group, and the only one among them with a rating above that of a private, had stood quietly by until the belligerent guard had threatened to bayonet Jamie. Rebel had quickly raised his crudely bound hands for permission to help, then stepped over to lift Jamie to his feet.

And when they had finished their one daily meal of a small metal cup of watery rice and finally got under way, Rebel had made sure that Jamie was in second place, close in behind him.

But Jamie hadn't been able to maintain the pace set by the guards. In spite of their hostility and constant prodding with brutal jabs from their rifle butts, he had begun to fall behind right away and ended up in last place by the time they arrived here at the opening in the jungle.

He managed to absorb the latest jolt and the sudden additional pain, and retain his balance though staggered by the blow. When he still made no effort to move, the fiery little guard stepped up behind him, raised his right foot to the small of Jamie's back and let out a shriek as he sent him sprawling forward.

Jamie landed face down as he slid in the stunted weeds and sand, about halfway to where the other prisoners had waited their turn to make their way across the dry creekbed.

He slowly drew in a breath as he pushed himself up onto his one knee and settled back on his heel, his useless leg folded under him. As he wiped the dirt and debris from his eyes and mouth with his bleeding hands, his head dropped slowly until his chin was resting on his chest again.

He was so ashamed, so thankful that Momma and Poppa didn't have to see him like this. They didn't have to witness his humiliation. They were so proud when they saw him off at the train station, in such high spirits when Momma hugged him and Poppa slapped him on the back while he shook his hand. They stood on the platform waving while the train left the station.

And Rosemary, dear, sweet Rosemary had smiled so

sweetly and snuggled so close the night before, while they talked of marrying when he got back home, after the war was over.

They had talked of having their own home there in the mountains, with a fireplace for the cool nights and a separate room for a nursery. He had held her close, feeling her warmth and gentle heartbeat while she described a white picket fence with flowers growing in front of it. Jamie had even promised to clear a piece of land for Rosemary to have her own vegetable garden, and build a chicken coop so they could have fresh eggs for breakfast and chicken and dumplings on Sunday.

The sharp tirade of the angry guard shattered Jamie's reverie and brought him back to the present. The sight of the caustic soldier in a terrible rage, brandishing his rifle at him again like he did this morning, made Jamie raise his head to look for Rebel or possibly one of the others, but four of the guards were gathered on this side of the streambed, facing toward him along the shallow bank, blocking his view of the other prisoners. They were being held at the far side of the jungle opening, in a tight line facing the lush foliage on the other side of the glade.

Jamie leaned forward on his hands, but his right leg, his entire body was so tired, so sore and full of pain that he slowly pushed himself back into a sitting position and let his head fall forward, his eyes downcast with his chin resting on his chest again. While his head moved slowly back and forth in defeat he was aware of the enraged guard's loud yelling, like that of a maniac, and then felt a sudden severely sharp pain in his chest.

It took a moment for Jamie to realize that he was now floating above it all, free of the wretchedness, free from all the pain and misery as he looked down and watched the surly guard place his booted foot on the chest of the emaciated body and yank his bayonet free.

He was still trying to grasp what had happened, still trying to fathom the bizarre turn of events when one of the four guards by the streambed let out a blood-curdling yell, brandishing his rifle as he charged across the short space, and plunged his bayonet into the midriff of the wasted body.

Jamie was horrified at the way his body was being mutilated and quickly went on the defensive, but the only thing that came to mind was the system he had worked out with Jodie, his younger brother, when they hunted in the mountains at home.

Jodie had been born with a crippled foot, one that required a built-up oversized shoe, and to keep a tab on him when they became separated in the forests where they hunted, they worked out a system using owl hoots. They had agreed, when out of sight of each other, to occasionally give one hoot just to let the other one know where they were, and two hoots if they needed help. The double hoot was to be accelerated in accordance with the severity of the emergency.

By the time Jamie was able to get his wits together, the other three guards from the streambed had each taken a turn to rush across and plunge their bayonets into the crumpled body.

The last of the four guards had just pulled his bayonet free and stepped back when the double hoot of an owl began to echo through the jungle. As the eerie double hoots seemed to move closer, coming much faster now, the five guards drew away from the disheveled body, frantically searching the dense growth surrounding the glade, and the bright skies above them.

They stumbled backward toward the dry streambed as the strange phenomenon suddenly seemed to draw closer and start emanating from the body they had violated there on the ground.

At the start of the eerie turbulence the remaining guards had moved the other eight prisoners closer to the jungle, away from the strange noise radiating from the far side of the streambed.

The last of them, both prisoners and guards, were just fading into the jungle when the short, muscular guard and the other four turned hurriedly, scattering sand and gravel as they ran from the streambed.

The onslaught of double hoots gradually slowed and faded away as the five guards hurried across the wide glade and plunged into the dense jungle growth without looking back.

Jamie was aware of the faint beacon off to his left and slightly behind, like the first rays of a false dawn, and from Grandpa's stories understood what it meant, but he would never be able to face Momma and Poppa, or Rosemary, especially Rosemary, if he allowed his very existence to end out here in the jungle. If he abandoned his broken body so far from home, so far from a proper burial in the quiet cemetery behind the steepled white church up there on the side of the mountain.

His soul could not even entertain the thought of ignoring his responsibility to them.

Chapter Two

As the thick foliage on the far side of the glade settled back into place and became still, as if it had never been disturbed, Jamie was oblivious to the returning sounds of the jungle.

The rapid chatter of a capricious monkey, the piercing call of a bird, the snorting of a wild boar somewhere in the area. He was so engrossed with the crumpled body sprawled in the weeds and stunted grass below him that he was slow to realize the urge to hurry was gone. The frantic need to keep up with the other prisoners had remained with his body.

Jamie's efforts to avoid the constant prodding of the guards since they had left the odorous camp site was only a memory now. Thoughts the open-ditch latrine, rotting garbage and crude bamboo cages had been replaced by the realization that he had, in fact, been abandoned in the jungle. But, somehow, it wasn't frightening anymore.

The resolve he had harbored to make it back home

after the war was still there, though. The promise to return to his family, and to Rosemary, had not been lost by the abrupt separation from his body. He was now obsessed with an obligation to watch over and protect his broken body until it could be recovered and sent back home.

He fervently looked down carefully examining the haggard body sprawled in the weeds. As he studied the rusted barbed wire restraining the bloody wrists, the odd angle of the left leg and the five bayonet holes in the blouse of the fatigues, he began to realize that all of his worldly troubles, the pain and anxiety, had remained with his body. He began to understand that he was no longer encumbered by the frailties, by the stringent limitations of a physical body, just his promise to his loved ones.

The realization of what had happened to him turned his thoughts back to the other prisoners. Jamie could envision them making their way slowly through the jungle. The guards, with their bayonet affixed rifles, were strung out along each side of the column, still aggressive, still eager for any chance to cruelly exercise their dominance.

He watched Rebel, still in the lead, so concerned and determined, carefully scrutinizing the jungle ahead of him. The man pushed aside a branch of heavy foliage, pointed with his bound hands to some kind of an obstacle on the ground, a fallen tree, small ravine or a low mound of loose leaves that could possibly be a shallow pit with bamboo stakes in it. Like the one he had inadvertently stepped into that night on patrol.

All of this sudden change in position would have been disturbing to Jamie if it hadn't been for Grampa Jordan, Jodie's namesake, who had always insisted that there were many souls of the departed still hanging around.

Souls who were reluctant to leave a loved one, souls that clung to a cherished place or possession, or simply felt the need to finish some obligation they had failed to complete before they died; before they had been so unexpectedly wrenched from the physical world.

Jamie was familiar with the acronym MIA/POW, but wasn't sure which, or even possibly that both might apply to him now, and Momma and Poppa be notified as such. It was disturbing enough to realize they would have to be told that he was a prisoner of war, and had been killed, but he didn't want the MIA part applied to him, didn't want them to be told that he had been lost altogether. They would never entertain the notion that he had deserted, it wasn't that.

He just didn't want to cause them any more hurt than was necessary because he was confident the military took care of its own, that it wouldn't be long before his body would be recovered and sent home.

There were reports of discoveries all the time. Even before he had been drafted there had been reports in the paper and on the radio, reports of the bodies of missing military personnel who had been located, whose bodies had been recovered and returned to their families.

He was determined to be here when they showed up, still had an obligation to Momma and Poppa and Jodie, and certainly to Rosemary, that would keep him right here until a recovery team showed up. He would make sure, somehow, that they found the hidden dog tag to properly identify his body and send it back home.

The thought of Rosemary brought an image of her kneeling at the altar in the hush of the early morning in the steepled white church, holding a loosely folded handkerchief to muffle her words while she murmured softly.

She had told him that she would ask God every day to watch over him while he was gone. She never referred to it as praying, just merely that she was talking to God, and would tell you that it needn't even be too loud for Him to hear her.

Jamie couldn't make out what she was saying but the very sight of her brought a resolve to get his body back home so she would know what happened. And a further resolve to be there when her time came, a resolve to be there to greet her and comfort her, to hold her close, or whatever they do up there, and try to make it up to her. It never entered his thoughts that she might possibly, in time, turn to someone else to build her a house and chicken yard, and help her with her vegetable garden.

As the image of Rosemary faded away his thoughts went back to that first night after his capture.

In the wee hours of that first night, when the guards had settled down, with some of them beginning to nod off after several bottles of that stuff they were drinking, the guy in the next cage quietly introduced himself as G.A. Said he was from Georgia, and whispered to Jamie to loosen the heel of one shoe enough to slip a dog tag under it. Jamie listened even though he had been a little skeptical at first, but when he had managed to glance around in the glare of the crudely rigged flood lights, had managed to see that there were other prisoners in similar cages, a cold fear gripped him as he began to realize the seriousness of his situation.

He had already removed his left shoe anyway, to do what he could to ease the pain in the festering wound in the calf of his leg. With the cage too shallow to stand in, or even wide or long enough for anything more than a fetal position, he had managed to hide the lone dog tag under the heel of his shoe. The one he had hidden in the waistband of his fatigues when he arrived over here from the States. The guards had taken away everything but his shoes and the clothes he was wearing before they bound his hands and forced him into the cramping, filthy cage.

An apprehension had plagued him from the time he began to understand that he had been captured by the enemy, was now a prisoner of war. It had brought on an ugly fear that he had failed them, that he might possibly disgrace his country even further, and his family, too.

The only thing anyone mentioned during his training about being captured was that he was to only give his name, rank and serial number. But the guy who gave that order had apparently never gone without food or water for any length of time, never had a thumb joint slowly crushed in a vise or a fingernail viciously twisted off with a pair of pliers.

When they questioned him, his name, rank and serial number was all he knew to give them. And they had apparently believed him, after a few brutal sessions, had finally believed that he honestly didn't know anything about the number of troops in the area, movements of personnel or equipment. They had only hit him a couple more times in his temple, then a couple of times in his kidneys with the heavy rubber truncheon, and finally finished by wrenching the nail from his left thumb.

He had thought that was bad until he started hearing the screams. Until he saw other prisoners with crippled hands, blood seeping from their ears and nose, had smelled their soiled clothing as they were herded past his cage, moving stolidly along, like zombies.

Then as they left the campsite the other day, or week, whenever it was, he had seen the ugliness of Rebel's bruises and his hand with the crushed thumb joint and bloody spots where the fingernails had been.

A loud snorting and a sudden violent disturbance down in the jungle to Jamie's left broke his musings. He watched the foliage as it trembled for a minute or so, aware from the sounds that an animal comparable to one of Grandpa's White Poland China boars was in conflict with something, even though he couldn't see anything through the dense growth. Then when the leaves and vines became quiet and settled back into place, he turned back to his body on the ground.

Grampa Jordan came to mind again as Jamie looked down, recalling how the solemn man had comforted Momma when Gramma Olga died.

While Jamie, still in grade school at the time, had stood obediently across the living room with Jodie, holding his little brother's hand, they had watched Grampa Jordan draw Momma to him and softly explain that her mother was in heaven now. Grampa had turned to the casket as he explained that Gramma Olga wouldn't want them to be sad, how she had risen to the place God had prepared for her, and that her body in the casket before them was merely an earthly garment. It was nothing more than a dress or coat that she had favored, and left for them to put away.

A twinge of guilt swept over Jamie at the sight of his body, at the condition of the earthly garment he had left for them. There was no way anyone could make his body presentable now, especially if it was very long before it was found. Maybe that was why they sometimes had a closed casket service for returned military people, or just a memorial service.

He hesitated at the thought of a memorial service, a funeral without a body. Momma and Poppa and Jodie, and Rosemary too, would never give up on him coming back until they had his body, or what was left of it. Until they understood what had happened, until they knew why he had not kept in touch, why he had not returned when the hostilities ended.

The thought brought an image of Momma and Poppa sitting at the old round oak kitchen table, where most all of their business problems and family calamities were handled.

Poppa was sitting straight up, his finger through the handle of his brown, ceramic coffee cup, looking down into it as though waiting for a possible answer as he usually did when things were beyond his control. Poppa was a God fearing man, but he sometimes had a problem with understanding God's way of doing things.

Momma sat across from him, her fisted left hand under her jaw supporting her head as she leaned over an open letter on the table before her. Several water spots glistened brightly on the Department of the Army letterhead as she sat quietly, fanning herself with a long white envelope bearing a military indicia.

A snorting sound, then a movement in the foliage brought Jamie's attention back to the ground below him. The large white boar strode from the foliage, chewing succulently on what appeared to be a piece of some kind of vine or root hanging from its mouth until Jamie saw the last foot or so of it thrash wildly one last time as the large hog greedily devoured it.

The hog's tusks, one protruding from each side of its lower jaw, continued to work up and down ravenously as it continued to chew. The beast ambled along, apparently aimlessly, until it spotted the body sprawled in the weeds and stunted grass.

Jamie watched in horror as the animal's small beady eyes studied the object on the ground out there before him while he finished chewing, slurping noisily as he swallowed.

Chapter Three

A shawl of despair and impotency settled over Jamie as he watched the huge boar finish chewing, smacking its mouth loudly for a moment, then move a step closer to the body. The animal was quite a bit larger than any of the hogs Grandpa Jordan ever had, even the two boars, a Poland China and a Duroc, and apparently more feral, too.

Grandpa had always moved the two rambunctious boars to a pen outside the hoghouse at farrowing time. He explained at first that the sows needed their own space to give birth and care for the new little piglets. Then in later years, after he and Jodie were old enough to understand and accept such things, Grandpa had explained that boar hogs had been known to kill the tiny newborn piglets by trampling them or rolling over on them, and in some instances they had even been known to eat them.

Jamie was still watching the boar, mulling over how he might possibly divert the animal from the body when his eye caught a slight movement in the leaves at the edge of the foliage, and heard a dull thud at the same time a deep grunt came from the big hog. He had not seen the long spear, like a javelin, until it was protruding from the boar's side, just behind its front leg. At the same moment he realized what had just happened, the hog's legs gave way and it went down heavily, then flopped over on its side with the bamboo shaft sticking straight up.

Two small brown-skinned natives in loin clothes and thatched conical hats stepped from the jungle and stopped, watching the fallen hog for a moment before they raised their voice back toward the jungle, then moved closer. Four additional natives, in similar dress and head coverings, stepped from the dense foliage carrying coils of sturdy braided vines, each of them with a large knife dangling from a shoulder sling.

The small group stepped to the rear of the fallen hog, unrolling their vine ropes and a short pole sharpened at each end, as though the operation had been rehearsed. They spread the animal's rear legs and inserted the pole between them, an end stuck through the tendons of each back leg just above the joints, then took their vine-ropes and fashioned a crude hanger. The younger appearing of the original two natives twisted the spear free as the other four dragged the heavy carcass over to a large tree at the edge of the clearing and threw one end of the vine-rope over a sturdy low limb. As the four hoisted the unwieldy body up from the ground the apparent older one of the first two natives drew his slender knife, with a slightly curved blade. As soon as the hog's head cleared the ground, he reached out and adeptly slit its throat all the way across and stepped aside from the spurting blood.

While the other natives prepared to cut open the hanging carcass and field dress it, the younger one with the spear moved back out of the way. He began cleaning the spearhead by grabbing handfuls of dried grass as he moved about, until he came upon the fatigue-clad body hidden by the tall grass. He stopped abruptly and drew back, staring wide-eyed as the clump of loose grass trickled loosely from his hand.

He slowly circled the body, using the upended spear as a staff. Then he stopped when the lone hoot of an owl echoed through the jungle. He listened intently for a moment, but the ominous owl hoot had faded away and his attention returned to the grim object on the ground before him. He circled the body a second time and stopped again.

After a long moment he turned toward the activity under the tree. When he saw his older cohort still standing back out of the way, occasionally pointing or giving advice, he glanced quickly at the crumpled body again, then turned and made his way through the tall grass. The man listened calmly as the excited younger one talked. He nodded a couple of times, then turned and followed when the younger one, still talking and pointing, made his way back over to where the body lay.

The older native circled the grim body slowly, closely noticing the odd position of the left leg, the rusty barbed wire binding the hands and the slits in the upper part of the uniform. After a moment he leaned down, reaching out reverently with one finger extended, and gently closed the sightless eyes of the fallen soldier.

He finally drew himself up and stood with closed eyes for a moment, turned to the younger man and began to talk, raising his eyes and arm to indicate well past where the other four natives were still busy with dressing out the body of the big boar. When he was through talking, and stepped back, the younger native nodded and picked up the spear, glanced quickly over at the body, then turned and left at a trot. He stolidly circled past the activity at the tree and disappeared into the jungle.

The older man continued to stand there in the tall grass, in sight of the crumpled body, and watched the other four natives fashion a net with their vine-ropes, cradle the pork carcass in it, then lift it between them and make their way into the jungle. He moved slowly through the tall grass to where they had dressed the boar and stopped, then turned back toward where the body lay. When he was satisfied he could see the area well enough, he began to fashion a small mat of dry grass and placed it at the base of the large tree, then hunkered down with his back against the gnarled trunk, facing toward the body. He placed his knife on the ground beside him, scooted around a little to get comfortable, then placed his arms across his knees in front of his face, drew in a breath and settled down to wait.

When one lone hoot of an owl broke the silence he didn't look up. It was soft and low, and somehow seemed to help him relax.

Chapter Four

Jamie seemed to rise higher and the scope of the area expand as he watched the young native with the spear enter the jungle, then the four natives carrying the large boar carcass as they, too, disappeared into the foliage. The native hunkered down under the big tree to guard Jamie's crumpled body sprawled out there in the grass and weeds didn't appear to be any farther away than he had been.

Jamie couldn't actually see the young native with the spear loping along through the jungle, just an occasional movement in the foliage. The lush green canopy stretched away below Jamie until he could see another clearing, seemingly larger than the one where his body lay.

The open expanse was taken up almost entirely by a village setting along the banks of a flowing stream. There were thatched huts and an open courtyard with smoldering cooking fires. The opening in the jungle and the remote settlement had come into view only a moment before the young runner with the spear emerged from the canopy of foliage and went directly to the larger hut located at the far end of the village.

The structure sat in an apparent position of prominence facing the open courtyard with its blackened caldrons. They sat on large rocks above the smoldering fires, surrounded by improvised skin-drying racks, with many smaller individual huts forming a perimeter for the village.

The runner had only been in the larger hut for a moment when he came back out and stepped aside for a taller, stately native clad in a full length robe of some kind of almost white animal skin. The collar and wide edging down the front of the robe were of leopard skin, his thatched headdress adorned with what looked like the upper part of a leopard's head.

The man stepped forward into the open courtyard and stopped, then raised his hands and clapped sharply two times. The short brown men began to emerge from their huts, slipping into their knife slings, donning their conical thatched hats and hefting their spears. While they congregated before their apparent chief, Jamie's attention returned to the native below, still hunkered down on his grass mat by the large tree.

Jamie was wary of the discovery of his body, and all the attention they were giving it, but he hadn't been happy with the body being unprotected, being left out in the open like that either. He was still trying to rationalize the situation when the native by the tree rocked forward and got up, then turned just as the taller native in the off-white, leopard skin trimmed robe emerged from the jungle. He stopped and set the end of his carved staff on the ground at arms length in front of him. A slight breeze stirred the trio of black feathers attached just below the crook at the top.

He and the native acknowledged each others presence with a nod. Then the native began talking as he raised his arm toward where the body lay. After a moment the chief nodded, picked up his scepter and they began to make their way slowly through the grass toward the body. The small band of natives who had emerged from the foliage behind the chief stood quietly with their supply of bamboo poles, braided vine-ropes and other paraphernalia.

Jamie was unsure of their intentions as he watched the chief and the native circle the body then step back and converse again. The chief leaned down a couple of times to examine the body more closely while they talked, then straightened up and raised an arm to summon the group waiting at the edge of the jungle.

As the group approached, the chief turned to the native who had waited by the tree, and began giving instructions. He, in turn, then began giving directions to the group as they put down their gear and listened for a moment, then began improvising a webbed cradle-like structure with the braided vine-ropes and bamboo poles.

The adept natives bent to the task of fashioning a stretcher of loosely woven vine-ropes between four of the bamboo poles, two on each side. When they finished, and the chief had nodded his approval, they carried it over to where the body lay. They hesitated to glance up at the sound of one lone owl hoot somewhere in the area, then placed the crude stretcher very reverently on the ground beside the body and stepped back.

The chief had looked up also to check the sky and surrounding trees until there was just the usual jungle sounds again, then stepped forward and gave directions for lifting the body onto the crude stretcher. When the natives had the body in place, the chief moved in and straightened the left leg alongside the other one, scowled at the cruelly bound hands as he made sure they were centered on the stomach and the head was resting solidly.

He started to straighten up but stopped, then leaned down hurriedly and again looked the body over, more carefully this time. After a moment he raised up, spoke briefly to the native who had waited by the tree and turned back to the body.

When the native then turned and began waving his arms toward the workers and motioning to the body on the woven stretcher, two of the natives scampered back to where they had left the other equipment they had brought with them and returned with two long handled torches.

Jamie became concerned and drew closer as four of the natives lifted the loosely woven stretcher to shoulder height while the two natives huddled together to ignite their torches.

One hoot of an owl echoed through the jungle, then faded away when the torches began to smolder instead of flare up, began to give off a pungent gray smoke instead of flames.

While the four natives held the stretcher aloft, the two natives with the smoking torches moved in, one on each side of the stretcher, and began moving their torch back and forth under the full length of the stretcher. They worked methodically, engulfing the body completely in the swirling smoke while the chief and the other native watched closely.

Jamie wasn't sure of what they were doing until he noticed the ants dropping from the body. Hundreds of large ugly ants were dropping through the wafting smoke and scurrying away into the weeds and grass.

When the chief was satisfied there were no more ants he motioned for them to lower the stretcher to waist level and stepped forward to examine the body again. While he moved along the stretcher, one of the natives came forward and handed him a crude brush fashioned from what looked like wild grass. The chief nodded as he took it then moved carefully along the length of the body, brushing and straightening the faded fatigues. He hesitated a moment at the hands, then carefully brushed the sleeves and pulled them right down to the barbed wire on the scarred wrists and moved on toward the feet.

Jamie watched skeptically while the chief finished tidying the body and stepped back. The four natives continued to hold the stretcher off the ground while the other natives retrieved their spears, knives and the other equipment they had brought with them, then the chief raised his scepter and stepped forward. The native who had waited by the tree fell in behind the chief, guiding those carrying the stretcher, with the working natives carrying their equipment bringing up the rear.

As the cortege made its way into the jungle, Jamie followed along, just above the canopy of leaves and vines, keeping the procession in sight through the breaks in the foliage.

Chapter Five

Jamie remained just above the edge of the plush green canopy as the procession emerged into the clearing. His apprehension began to ease at the sight of the chief walking solemnly, so concerned as he glanced back occasionally. And, too, the native that had waited by the tree was walking sideways, sometimes even backward, guiding the four natives bearing the improvised stretcher. Jamie still had no idea of what they had in mind, but the sight of his body being borne so piously relieved some of his anxiety.

He hadn't been happy about his body being exposed there in the weeds and grass where the guards had left it, open to the elements and whatever else might come along. He had really had no choice, but now, with these people's kindness, saving the body from the large boar. He was aware that they might have just been out tracking the boar for its meat, but he was grateful for their concern, and they did get rid of all those ants.

The sight of the body being handled so carefully on

the stretcher was comforting, until he saw the small group of women gathering around. They stood back as the four natives lowered the stretcher onto four upright waist high stanchions in the ground. It was beside a second larger thatched structure on a slight hill behind the Chief's hut.

A pile of some kind of large green leaves on the ground near where the four stanchions stood had escaped Jamie's notice until he saw several younger natives, mere boys, emerge from the jungle. They were laden with additional leaves and dropped them onto the pile. As the boys turned and went back into the heavy foliage, each carrying a machete almost as big as he was, the women began to gather around the stretcher.

Two of the women stepped over by the pile of leaves, each with a grass brush in her hand. They waited while the other women gathered around the stretcher, four on each side, and slowly rolled the body onto its left side. The four women on the far side held the body in place while the other four turned back and forth taking leaves from the other two women as they cleaned them with their crude brushes.

Jamie moved closer as the women carefully placed the large leaves in a row under the body. When they had proficiently woven the stems and serrated edges of the large overlapping leaves together, forming a thin cushioning pallet, they smoothed it out to their satisfaction and all eight of them then slowly lowered the body back and raised it onto its right side. The first four women then held the body in place while the other four fashioned a connecting pallet on the other side of the stretcher.

When they had completed the full pallet the body was lowered onto its back again. The women at the foot on each side began placing large leaves over the feet and legs, weaving them together as they went, forming a cocoon of sorts as they worked their way up the body.

Two of the women, one on each side at the head, carefully brushed the face, adjusted the collar and shoulders of the fatigue blouse, then took a minute to select one of the large leaves. They shook it vigorously for a moment, brushed both sides and gently placed it over the shrunken face.

The women inspected their work carefully when they were finished, then picked up the few leaves that were left and placed them loosely along the top of the concealed body and stepped back into a group.

As the last woman from the far side made her way toward the head of the stretcher, she stopped and bent down to pick up something from the ground. Jamie only got a quick glimpse as she closed her hand around it and continued along the stretcher to join the other women where they waited in the shade at the edge of the canopy of foliage.

Jamie had forgotten all about the delicate little gold bracelet he had bought at the PX a couple of days after he had arrived over here. He didn't particularly like the idea of substituting a heart for the word 'love', but it was already there so he just had them engrave his and Rosemary's names, one on each side of the little heart.

She wouldn't mind, he was sure, but he hadn't had a chance to wrap and mail it before he went on patrol that night. He hadn't wanted to let the bracelet out of his sight, and even when he was captured he had kept it hidden even though they took everything else.

He was so engrossed in watching the woman with Rosemary's bracelet, trying to rationalize that it was probably better for someone to have it than for it to have fallen from his pocket sooner and been lost in the jungle somewhere along the way, when he suddenly realized the chief was approaching.

The man stopped and nodded to the group then moved slowly along the stretcher, closely examining the women's handiwork. He spent a long moment at the head, then nodded his approval as he turned to face the group of women again.

Almost before he turned the woman with the bracelet approached him with her hand out. She nodded toward the ground beneath the stretcher as she talked, apparently explaining what if was and where she had found it.

As she returned to her place in the group of women, the chief examined the bracelet closely for a minute. He wiped it slowly along the suede-like sleeve of his coat, studied it for another moment then dropped it into an inner pocket and turned to the four men approaching the corners of the stretcher.

The chief waited while they lifted the stretcher and steadied it between them, then led them around to the front of the tall hut where several other men stood holding the heavily thatched double doors open.

Jamie drifted in right above the chief, following along as the man stopped to point to a vacant shelf of fresh bamboo poles. While the men raised the stretcher and slid it onto the shelf and secured it with pieces of woven-vine ropes, Jamie hovered just above his body in its cocoon as he glanced around. It appeared to be a mausoleum of sorts, and apparently only for persons of some prominence. There were not that many shelves, and the cocoons on the shelves each had some sort of object perched on top of it. A leopard skin trimmed hat, a cluster of black feathers or something that looked like an animal skin satchel.

Small tendrils of some kind of vapor hovered above several of the cocoons. It looked like smoke, probably to repel the ants, until he began to recognize faint images in each of them that apparently matched the body in the cocoon below. It was frightening until he realized that was probably how they were seeing him now.

He appreciated that his body was out of harms way, and protected from the elements, but he couldn't leave it here like this. Wouldn't even consider the thought of Momma and Poppa and Jodie and certainly Rosemary, never knowing what happened to him. He was aware of the urgency emanating from the faint light off to his left, but he would have to wait here to make sure his body was found and sent back home to be buried in the cemetery behind the church up there on the side of the mountain.

Chapter Six

Jamie looked down at the woven cocoon enclosing his body, and the surroundings, so foreign to the life he had known. He began to wonder what the Army might think when they found him. The dog-tag was still in his shoe so there would be no problem with identification, but how would they know what happened, know why he ended up here like this? Surely they would find out that he had been taken prisoner, would know that he hadn't just run off somewhere, hadn't deserted.

He wanted to believe that when the rest of the squad had returned from patrol that night without him the lieutenant would have sent out a search party that would probably have found the pit, since it wasn't hidden anymore. They would surely have seen the blood on the leaves and the discards from the snakebite kit. He doubted there would have been any footprints left in the rotting vegetation on the ground, any kind of a trail they could follow. The night rains would have already taken care of that.

When they questioned the rest of the patrol, and the members of the search party they would have no choice but to list him as a POW. He had never given anyone any trouble, given anyone reason to believe he was unhappy or resentful. Had never given anyone reason to think he was anything other than a dedicated soldier, content with fulfilling his obligation to his country and his loved ones back home.

The night he stepped into the hole that was hidden by the flimsy cover of loose leaves, and felt the sudden sharp sting in the back of his leg, the first thing that came to mind was all the stories of the jungle snakes; stories that had been foisted off on the new recruits and other arriving replacement personnel.

The only snakes he and Jodie ever had to worry about in the forests at home where they hunted were the poison ones, the rattlesnakes and copperheads. Jamie was not exactly afraid of snakes, but respectful enough of them to know that when you had been bitten by a poisonous one you needed to tend to it right away. And the army apparently agreed because they had furnished each one of them with a snakebite kit, and instructed them in its proper use.

Jamie dwelled on the thought of the medic's deceptive spiel on the consequences of failing to use the snakebite kit immediately and properly. The city boys, who had probably never even seen a snake, other than in a zoo, grinned skeptically as the doc warned that if they did not use the kit soon enough, and the poison got into their blood stream, they would be subject to a series of antitoxin shots.

Then all levity vanished when the doc added, as if it were an after thought, that the special serum for untended bites of most jungle snakes had to be injected directly into the left testicle with a square needle.

Jamie had already taken his snakebite kit out that night when he discovered the hole in his pants leg above his combat boot, and wasn't really sure that it was a snakebite, but treated it as though it were, anyway.

He had only grunted when he stumbled, when his foot went through the fragile cover, and he had tried to suppress that. He was well aware of the need for stealth and the safety of maintaining contact on patrol, but instinct, and all the talk about snakes had dictated that the injury, whatever it was, needed immediate attention. Despite his panic at the silent attack and the sharp pain in his leg he had managed to clean the wound and dress it, as well as he could in the dark, and put his shoe back on. Then when he started to get up, he suddenly realized the figures with rifles who had quietly moved in and surrounded him wasn't his patrol unit.

His memory of the painful, torturing trek through the dank, smelly jungle for the rest of that night and most of the next day, without food and very little water, had already begun to fade away when one of the outside doors of the burial hut opened.

Jamie watched the Chief enter solemnly, accompanied by the native who had waited by the tree. The man followed the Chief along, almost ritualistic, carefully carrying a small bamboo cross embedded upright in what looked like a piece of flat brown rock. Rosemary's bracelet was draped around the short top post, dangling brightly from the little crossbar.

When they reached the shelf where his body had been placed, the Chief stopped while the man moved past him and placed the improvised adornment on the cocoon, made sure it was centered and resting solidly and stepped back. Both of the men raised their solemn faces skyward while the Chief made a short oratory, almost like a chant. Then the two of them turned and left, pulling the door closed behind them.

Jamie moved closer to examine the small gadget. It sort of reminded him of the way the bracelet had been displayed at the PX on a clear plastic stand. It had apparently been polished, the way it glistened in the subdued light here in the thatched hut. The little heart with his and Rosemary's name engraved on each side of it wouldn't mean anything to these people, especially out here in the jungle. Then at the thought that he couldn't understand the chief or the natives, he had to concede that it would mean nothing more to these people than a trinket, just a shiny bauble.

But he realized that it was probably meant merely as a momento of the person entombed there, like the tokens on the other bodies resting here in this jungle mausoleum. He could only guess that each one was a favorite thing or symbol of the departed person. From what he could see they must have all been prominent people. One wore a conical straw hat with the upper part of a leopard's head on it, like the current Chief's, another with a larger bamboo cross supporting a necklace of some kind of teeth. He studied it a moment before he realized the thin, curved objects weren't teeth, but toenails. There was enough to be a complete set from one animal; some kind of jungle cat.

The more he looked around the more he realized how out of place he and his body were. He appreciated that his body was protected now, but it didn't fit in, couldn't stay here.

Jamie glanced off to his left at the faint light in the distance, as he thought about what Grandpa Jordan had told him and Jodie about spirits hanging around for some reason. It might take the military awhile to find his body, but he would be here when they did.

Chapter Seven

Time had lost all meaning for Jamie as he hovered above the quiet thatched mausoleum in the jungle, watching over his body. The activities of the small village, as well as the surrounding area, changed very little from one day to the next.

After some time it began to get monotonous watching the natives. The women spent a part of each day washing garments and other stuff at the edge of the river and draped them over crude racks to dry in the sun, much like those holding the skins. They also tended the steaming caldrons, chopping up meat of some kind and what looked like jungle roots and vegetables at the open work tables, then stirring as they dropped the mixture into the steaming pots.

The men made daily treks into the jungle and dugout canoe trips on the river to replenish the village larders. In between they spent their time sharpening spearheads and knives, fashioning additional spears from saplings and bamboo, as well as repairing and reweaving their fishing nets.

Even the children worked, except the babies who were carried in a crude sling on their mother's back. The girls helped with the laundry and cooking and the boys went into the jungle to gather wood for the cooking fires, thatch for the repair and maintenance of the village structures.

Jamie began to realize that the natives existence was really not that much different than his own life had been at home before he had been drafted. They appeared to be a caring people, content with their lot, comfortable with life here in the jungle.

Their concern for his body was appreciated, but he still wanted it to go home. He wanted it to be with his family and friends, and yes, with Rosemary. She would probably never know what actually happened, but at least she would know why he hadn't come back to her.

Life was continuing at its usual pace one morning when their long dugout turned hurriedly in from the river and one of the younger natives jumped into the shallow water and splashed ashore even before the vessel glided onto the sandy shore and stopped. The boy ran up the slight incline of the bank, turned left through the village and continued on to the Chief's hut. He stopped for a minute at the front step to catch his breath, then crossed   the small porch, pushed the door open and went in.

After a moment the Chief stepped out of his hut, pulling on his official coat and hat, then raised his hands and clapped them together sharply. As the men in the compound stopped what they were doing and gathered around, the Chief handed a small object to the native who had waited by the tree when they found the body, then turned to address the men who were gathering before him.

When the native with the small object headed for the

burial hut, Jamie followed along. The sudden excitement had whetted his curiosity, but he was more concerned with the native's errand to the mausoleum.

As Jamie rose above the roof of the burial hut to watch the native enter, he noticed there was a continuing movement in the jungle foliage and it was rapidly approaching the clearing.

Jamie watched the native enter the hut and go to where his body rested. The man reached up and covered Rosemary's bracelet with a small replica of a well-worn thatched hat, made sure it was in place, then turned and went back out to join the group in front of the Chief.

The Chief had no more than finished his instructions and motioned the group back to their duties and went back into his own hut when a group of nine Oriental soldiers and their leader stepped out of the jungle. They were all in forest green battle dress, each carrying a rifle with bayonet affixed, and crossed the clearing directly to the Chief's hut.

The leader of the patrol shouted as he stepped up on the small porch, then started kicking at the door just as the Chief pulled it open and stepped out to face them.

After much bluster, loud talk and arm waving between the Chief and group's leader, one of the soldiers raised his rifle and stepped forward menacingly. He rudely forced the Chief, at bayonet point, back into his hut, then pulled the door shut and turned rigidly to take up the position of guard.

The rest of the patrol fanned out to do a brusque search of the small village. They went arrogantly through each hut, shoving everything around roughly, then left doors open on leaving, some even hanging askew.

Cooking kettles, work tables and drying racks were overturned, clothes and drying skins slashed. Then, ignoring the burial hut, they began to regroup again at the edge of the jungle.

The body of the patrol was oblivious to the antics and vulgar laughter of the three soldiers who were gesturing bawdily as they shoved a sobbing preteen girl back and forth between them, tearing at her clothes as they went. The rest of the group of soldiers milled around. Some smoking, others resting, squatting with their backs to a tree, apparently uninterested and unconcerned with the lewd activity of the three boisterous soldiers.

Jamie didn't recognize any of them. Asian soldiers all looked pretty much alike to him, but he was repulsed by both them and their leader's indifference to the plight of the young girl.

As he watched vengefully, Jamie noticed the thin wisp of vapor that had hung near the ceiling over the body with the necklace of animal claws resting on it. It had begun to move, swirling suddenly as it became larger, wafted away through the thatched wall and settled to the ground like a large dust devil, in full view of the three soldiers.

Two of them were now holding the hysterical girl on the ground while the third one had begun to undo the front of his pants as the swirling vapor came to rest before them. It whirled even faster as it grew, then the vapor quickly faded away to reveal a short muscular native, his long spear and colorful shield slung across his back. There was a small bone through his flat nose and a necklace of animal claws around his neck.

The phantom warrior dipped a slim dart into a small pouch on a strap hanging diagonally from his shoulder and inserted the dripping projectile into his blowgun. As he raised his sullen eyes and the long bamboo tube, the soldier that had been opening his pants had drawn back with his knees together, holding his clothes and himself protectively, but had failed to contain the blossoming wet stain at the crotch of his pants.

The other two guards had abandoned the girl, as well as their weapons, and scurried away, on hands and knees, to the protection behind one of the overturned caldrons.

The appearance, the very sight of the warrior fascinated Jamie. He had always been skeptical of Grandpa Jordan's tale about Oscar Hutchens, who had been killed in the first World War and was buried somewhere in France. Grandpa reveled in telling the story of how Oscar had suddenly materialized behind his wife one day while Silas Muldoon from the bank in town was threatening to foreclose on her farm if she refused to sell the property to him. Grandpa always chuckled as he described how Silas had blanched and slunk away. And how the mighty Mr. Muldoon managed to find a legitimate excuse to avoid Mrs. Hutchens completely after that.

As the swirling vapor reappeared and engulfed the warrior, it whirled even faster as it rose and wafted the apparition back to the burial hut. The sobbing girl sat up slowly and looked around, then got up and gathered up her clothes, watching the cowering soldier warily as she crossed to one of the huts and went inside.

The other two soldiers waited a long moment before cautiously crawling from behind the large caldron, ignoring the girl completely as they retrieved their weapons, then joined the other one who was still adjusting his soiled pants. The three of them finally made their way as inconspicuously as possible across the compound and merged quietly with the rest of the group.

After some heated discussion and instructions, and a check of their weapons, the group made their way back across the clearing to where they had come and disappeared into the jungle.

Chapter Eight

Jamie's loathing for the indifference of the soldiers, the indecency of the three in particular, took his attention back to the sadistic guards who had marched him and the others through the jungle.

His concern for the other prisoners took him back to the opening in the jungle where he had last seen them, then moved him along the broken jungle growth until he came to a bamboo and barbed wire stockade that appeared to be more than just a temporary camp. It was on the banks of a river, somewhat larger than the one by the village here where his was. There was an old wooden dock projecting out from the bank, with a sizeable, scruffy looking boat, like a small freighter, moored alongside, gently riding the river's sluggish current.

There were no bamboo cages in the camp, like the ones where he had been held after he was captured, but there were several strands of barbed wire stretched tightly above the high bamboo walls. Instead of cages there were heavy wooden short posts imbedded in the ground, with a sturdy crossbar for holding prisoners in a sitting position with their arms extended out on each side. None of the prisoners restrained in them were familiar.

He could, however, recognize a few in the guarded line of prisoners waiting at a table in the open compound. Two larger men in black uniforms and knee-high black leather boots were replacing the prisoner's barbed wire wrist restraints with metal handcuffs and installing heavy shackles on their ankles that had a short length of chain between them.

Rebel and GA were standing just inside the locked gate, closely guarded by two of the Oriental soldiers in green uniforms, their rifles held at the ready. The barbed wire on their wrists had now been replaced with metal handcuffs. Their ankles bore the heavy shackles with a short length of chain between them.

The others from the group he had been in were still waiting in line at the table, guarded by several of the Oriental soldiers. The same two of the Caucasian men in black uniforms were at the table, replacing the barbed wire at their wrists, and installing heavy leg shackles with the short hobbling chain between them.

As Jamie watched the activity, several more men in the same black uniforms came out on deck of the old boat and started rigging a tent-like cover above the starboard deck.

They attached one side of a large faded tarpaulin along the eave of the superstructure then stretched it across the deck to several posts rising from the rusty scuppers at the outer edge of the deck. When they had finished installing the canopy they checked it briefly, tugging at it in several places, then moved over to the railing and stood there in the shade of their creation, talking quietly as they brought out cigarettes and lit them.

All conversation stopped, however, as they watched two of the guards in green uniforms, rifles with bayonets affixed, come marching stiffly down from the stockade and take up a position on the dock, one on each side of the small wooden gangway.

There was no recognition, or any attempt at communication between any of the soldiers. The two Orientals in green uniforms stood rigidly in their positions on each side of the gangway, and the other larger men in black uniforms, the ones gathered on the deck of the boat, continued to smoke and talk quietly among themselves.

When the last of the group of prisoners had been refitted with the metal restraints, a squad of Oriental guards in green uniforms belligerently lined them up and marched them out of the stockade and headed them noisily toward the dock. The rambunctious guards shouted rudely and prodded the men with their rifle butts, even threatening to use their bayonets on the slower of the hobbled prisoners.

When the prisoners arrived at the dock the two guards began to shout boisterously, shoving and jabbing as they marshalled the prisoners into a single line at the gangway.

The group of soldiers in black uniforms dropped their cigarette butts into the river and moved toward the gangway as they watched the egotistical performance on the dock.

Jamie didn't know the nationality of the men waiting on the boat and the two inside the camp that had done the reshackling. He didn't get the idea they were Americans, but they were certainly not Oriental. They were much larger and seemed to be more confident, not so hostile, and had much lighter skin than the Oriental soldiers.

Jamie had never been able to identify a person's nationality, but the men did kind of resemble that group of entertainers he had seen in the circus several years ago when Momma and Poppa took him and Jodie to the circus when it was at the Fairgrounds. The guys in the black uniforms and leather boots had the same appearance and mannerisms as the troupe of jugglers, particularly the big guy with the full beard and dancing bear.

Jamie watched solemnly as the Oriental guards hustled the prisoners up to the rickety gangway. They moved the shackled men along one at a time, shouting and rudely shoving them along with their rifle butts then he noticed how considerate the other soldiers were of the prisoners when they finally reached the boat deck.

The soldiers in black uniforms carried no weapons or raised their voice as they greeted each prisoner. They positioned them quietly along the steel bar at the base of the superstructure, then leaned down and quietly secured their leg chains to the bar.

When all of the prisoners has been seated and secured to the steel bar, two of the soldiers on the boat pulled in the small gangway. The Oriental soldiers sullenly unwound the fore and aft hawsers mooring the boat, let them fall into the water and stepped back. There were no goodbyes or farewell waves as the boat started backing away from the dock.

Jamie watched forlornly while the two guards pulled in the hawsers as the boat turned slowly, then, with a puff of gray smoke, began to make its way down the muddy river, picking up speed as it went. He hadn't really known any of the prisoners, or even seen any of them before he was captured, but he wished them well. The war was over for him, but the Lord only knew when, if ever, it would be over for them.

He sighed as he thought of Rosemary and Momma and Poppa. Yes, and Jodie. It really wasn't over for him yet, either. He still had the going home part to do that he had promised.

Chapter Nine

The weathered old boat with no markings, and flying no flag, faded into the distance, leaving just a seemingly deserted prison camp on a muddy river in the noisy jungle. Jamie's concern for the other prisoners became more acute, as severe as his obsession of seeing that his own body would be found and returned home. Of seeing that his body would be returned to his family, so they would know why he hadn't returned and give it a proper burial in the quiet cemetery behind the family church.

His sentiments toward the other prisoners being returned to their homes and loved ones were almost as strong as the obligation he felt toward his own body. Even though he had not had much of a chance to know any of them very well, it bothered him to see them being taken even farther away from their families and loved ones. He hadn't had much of a chance to know Rebel and GA, but he would never forget their kindnesses. It hurt him to think of what they might still have to endure.

The thought of home took him back to the only place

he had ever known, the large house up there on the side of the mountain, at the edge of the forest, and his old room on the second floor, overlooking the wide picturesque valley below.

The familiar scene unfolded before him, fluffy white clouds in the bright blue sky above the high mountains with their green forests. He drifted easily into his old room, and was surprised to see Rosemary sitting in his chair. The big fan-back rocker that had belonged to Grandpa Jordan.

She leaned against the sturdy left arm, solemnly holding his last letter open before her, her eyes heavy as she read. There had been other letters while he was in training, at least weekly, but with all the orientations and other activity when he got over here he had only managed to write her the one.

While he watched her read, she ignored a large tear that spilled over the lower lid of her left eye and made its way down her cheek. When it stopped at her chin and just hung there, he watched for a moment before he noticed a little yellow ribbon pin on the collar of her white blouse. It and the tear glinted brightly as she rocked slowly back and forth.

After a moment, when she had finished reading, she let the rocker become still as she carefully refolded the letter and slipped it back into the envelope. She sat there for a long moment, looking down at the envelope, running her fingertips slowly back and forth over the APO return address. Then she settled back in the chair, pressing the letter possessively to her breast.

Her features became grave as she closed her eyes and began to rock slowly again. She understood the APO in the return address, Jamie had explained all that while he was home on leave, but it didn't help her to know where he had mailed the letter from, and certainly gave no indication as to where he was now.

Jamie drifted down from the ceiling as he watched her, moving close enough to sense the heat of her body, then hovered even closer when he began to pick up her scent. She had always smelled so clean and fresh, like a woman. She had never used perfume even though he had given her a small bottle for Christmas while he was home on training leave last year. She had thanked him with that impish little kiss on the cheek and said that she was going to put it away for now because it smelled like something a married woman would wear.

He held back, stifling the urge to kiss her on the cheek. He wished he had paid more attention when Grandpa Jordan talked about the souls of people who had died. About their hanging around to protect someone they loved, or to finish some kind of business.

According to Grandpa, Mr. Hutchens had only appeared to protect his wife from Mr. Muldoon's threats, and had apparently made no effort to touch his wife, or even let her see him. And the native chief had only appeared before the three soldiers to protect the girl. No one else acted like they had seen anything unusual.

Jamie continued to hover close to Rosemary as she rocked quietly in the big chair, his last letter held tightly in her hands. He wanted her to know that he hadn't deserted her, wanted her to know that he was there, but he didn't want to frighten her.

They had often sat and talked on the sofa downstairs in front of the big fireplace, talked and made plans for their future, then cuddled together when they didn't feel the need to talk anymore. She would settle her head on his shoulder and kiss him lightly on the cheek. Then she would smile without opening her eyes and snuggle even closer. He could still remember the sensation of her soft breath on his neck.

He slowly surveyed the room. It somehow didn't look

so drab anymore, not like it was when he was there. The framed picture of him in uniform that he had them make at the PX, the one he had sent to Momma and Poppa was sitting there on the dresser, and the picture of him and Rosemary, the one they had made on his short leave before he shipped out, was on the small chest by the bed. And Rosemary's bedspread, the purple and white one with the crazy pattern, she said it was called a drunkard's something, was on the bed.

The curtains were different, more frilly and tied back, and the pictures her father had taken of their graduation, pictures that belonged to her, were now framed and hanging on the wall. And the large cedar chest at the foot of the bed was the one he had refinished for her; the one that had belonged to her grandmother.

With the thought that she had apparently moved into his room, he began to feel even more possessive, and hovered down again to kiss her on the cheek, but stopped. He didn't want to frighten her, and wasn't really sure if he could still do something like that, anyway.

He didn't know how Mr. Hutchens or the native Chief had managed to appear like they did. He had no idea of how to do it, and didn't feel it was necessary, anyway. He just wanted to sneak a kiss to let her know he was concerned about her without her knowing he was there.

Jamie moved away from her, deep in thought as he drifted upward and just hung there below the ceiling. Grandpa Jordan had talked like a soul drifting around out there could do just about anything they wanted to, but he hadn't gone into any detail. He had not mentioned anything about two people in love that had been separated like this before they could really share their love. He hadn't mentioned anything about the possibility of a soul having any kind of connection to the loved one that had been left behind.

Iranian opposition leaders are relocated

Two Iranian opposition leaders have been moved secretly from their homes, where they had been under virtual house arrest for calling on supporters to protest against the government, a rights group said Sunday.

Mir Hossein Mousavi and Mehdi Karoubi had been forced to stay in their homes in the capital of Tehran for more than two weeks. Mousavi's daughters said on the Kaleme website that they had been prevented from approaching the house since Feb. 14.

The International Campaign for Human Rights in Iran quoted an "informed source" as saying Mousavi and Karoubi, along with their wives, had been moved from their homes to a "'safe house' in an area close to Tehran."

Irish party hopes to get new bailout deal

THE NEWSMAKER

Iraqi Cabinet told: Reform or else

Prime Minister Nouri al-Maliki on Sunday gave Iraqi ministers a 100-day ultimatum to step up reforms or face the loss of their jobs amid nationwide

protests against corruption and poor basic services. Thousands of Iraqis took to the streets Friday to protest against shortages of electricity, food rations and jobs, and called for some provincial officials to step down. More protests took place Sunday.

Tea Party Patriots

Chapter Ten

An urgent sensation brought Jamie back to the tranquil burial hut in the noisy jungle. He watched anxiously while two unarmed officers carrying briefcases, being escorted by a small squad of soldiers that were armed, entered the village compound. The armed soldiers carried their weapons more in a manner of protectiveness of the two unarmed officers than any show of belligerence or aggression.

Jamie's trepidation was slowly replaced by a warm glow when he began to recognize the familiar markings on the uniforms, and realize that they were American.

The group made their way cautiously across the open area to the Chief's hut, the armed soldiers on the alert as they separated to move along each side of the two officers with their briefcases. While the two officers approached the Chief's door and knocked modestly, making their presence known, the others formed a protective half circle across the front of the large hut with their weapons held at the ready.

The door was finally opened by the Chief's assistant.

The native glanced slowly around at the squad deployed in front of the hut. He stepped back inside for a moment, then returned and invited the two officers to enter.

Jamie drifted into the large hut while the Chief welcomed the two officers and motioned for them to have a seat at the large table in the middle of the main room. The older one of the two American officers apparently had some knowledge of the Chief's language. He and the Chief conversed hesitantly for a moment, gesturing and nodding, then the two officers placed their briefcases on the large table and quietly took a seat.

As the senior officer continued to nod, looking up at the Chief as he talked, he opened his briefcase and took out a large, buff colored envelope. He placed it on the table before him, still talking to the Chief as he unwound the little string tie.

Jamie moved in closer when the soldier removed a picture of an airplane and handed it to the Chief. Jamie wasn't that familiar with airplanes, especially combat planes, but the Chief apparently recognized this one from the way he nodded as he reached out and took it. He turned to the light coming from the opening under the hut's eave to study the picture.

The Chief calmly examined the picture for a long moment, giving a slight nod now and then, and finally turned and motioned to his assistant. The shorter man stepped to the Chief's side and leaned over the table to examine the picture. The man nodded slowly as he followed the Chief's finger, calling attention to several decals and markings on the plane. They studied what they could see of the colored insignias and emblems on the fuselage, wings and tail section, talking knowingly as they nodded back and forth, then the Chief turned to the two officers and raised his arm, pointing as he spoke.

While the Chief continued to point as he eagerly explained, holding the two officer's rapt attention, the younger officer fumbled blindly as he opened his briefcase and took out a folded map. He unfolded it slowly and spread it on the table, then when the Chief had finished, the other officer nodded toward the map, motioning for the Chief to join him as he leaned down over it.

When the Chief moved warily closer and leaned down, squinting his confusion with the colorful piece of paper, the senior officer put his finger on the site of the village where they were and began to explain.

As the officer talked, moving his finger north along the small river that ran by the village, in the direction the Chief had been pointing, he explained the elevations and other landmarks shown on the map. The Chief followed along, listening attentively, nodding now and then as if he really understood, then reached out quickly and put his finger on the spot on the map where the officer said it showed an appreciable elevation.

The Chief held his finger firmly on that spot on the map while he spoke eagerly to the officer, cutting his eyes occasionally toward the picture of the plane on the table, then nodding to the officer as if to confirm what he had just said.

 When the Chief had finally managed to connect the place on the map with the picture of the plane on the table next to the map, the senior officer turned quickly to the other one.

The younger officer pushed his chair back as he listened, then got up and crossed to the door. He stepped outside and stopped, glancing around as if looking for someone in particular. After a moment he raised his arm and motioned to the soldier waiting in the shade of a small tree at the edge of the jungle, the one with the small back pack.

As the soldier approached him, the officer began to explain. The soldier listened attentively while the man briefed him, then when the officer motioned toward the door of the hut, the soldier slung his rifle over his left shoulder as he was ushered into the Chief's hut.

When they reached the table where the other officer and the Chief were waiting, the soldier unslung his rifle and leaned it against one of the chairs, then removed his back pack and placed it on the table. He quickly raised a thin, telescoping antenna, removed a handset and gave the crank on the side of the backpack several sharp turns. He raised the handset to his ear, in position to respond and waited a moment, then placed the handset on the table again and gave the crank several more vigorous turns.

The second time there was a response. The little green light on top of the backpack by the antenna came on. The soldier raised the handset into position again and spoke several words into the phone, then nodded and turned to pass the handset to the senior officer waiting to talk and give the coordinates of the plane's location on the map.

Jamie became excited at the thought of the officer being able to contact someone, being able to summon more American military personnel to the area.

He had lost all track of time, but he had been here long enough. He was grateful to the natives for their concern for his body, appreciative of all their kindnesses, but he was also glad that his body was going to be found. Glad that it would soon be on its way home.

Chapter Eleven

While the senior officer thanked the Chief and continued to converse with him, the radioman closed his phone pack, slid his arms into the shoulder straps and jostled it into position on his back. When he had it in place and buckled to suit him, he picked up his rifle and headed for the door.

The other officer had been folding the map and carefully returning the picture of the plane to its envelope. He closed the flap by winding the string around the two little paper tabs, then opened his briefcase and carefully positioned them inside.

Jamie hovered above them, watching closely, warmly content with the feeling he was part of the U.S. Army again. It had taken them long enough to get here, but he had never doubted them for a minute. He patiently watched the two officers close their briefcases, express their gratitude to the Chief again as they shook hands, then pick up their briefcases. They each gave the Chief a quick two-finger salute and turned toward the door.

Outside, with the reappearance of the two officers, the troops began to gather around. When the senior officer had briefed them on his meeting with the Chief, and answered their questions concerning the plane, they formed into two lines, one on each side of the officers. The group moved across the compound, in the direction of where the officer had reported the location of the downed plane and entered the jungle.

Jamie reluctantly watched them go. He wasn't sure if the Chief, in all of his conversation with the officers, had mentioned recovering his body or even that it was here in the village.

He wanted to believe the Chief had, and as soon as they recovered the pilot, or the plane, or whatever it was they were after, they would come back for his body. He was aware that the Army operated strictly on written orders, and by priority, and still believed the recruiting posters he had seen that the Army takes care of its own.

With the onset of a distant, cadenced throb, Jamie rose above the tree tops and turned in that direction. He saw the small dot appear on the horizon, then gradually grow until it took the shape of a helicopter. It grew larger as it skimmed along, just above the dense jungle foliage, zigzagging slowly as it came, apparently searching for some sign of the downed plane that had been reported.

The chopper finally slowed and circled back, then came to a stop and hovered. After a long moment it sent two men down, one at a time on a cable. The cable was retracted after the second man was on the ground, and the aircraft began to slowly circle the immediate area. It made a couple of turns before it located an opening in the foliage that was large enough to accommodate the expanse of its rotors, and gently settled to the ground.

Jamie moved a little closer, enough to see several men emerge from the aircraft as its motors whined down. The whirling motion had created turbulence in the soggy ground cover and surrounding foliage before it slowed to a lazy turn.

The men seemed to ignore the downdraft and spiraling debris as they dropped from the body of the plane and turned back to retrieve their weapons and other equipment. They also took several machetes from the chopper, and what looked like a pruning saw, then formed up and headed off through the jungle toward the site of the downed plane.

Jamie followed along, watching the men hack and saw their way through the small trees and vines toward the rocky slope where the crumpled plane was all but swallowed up by the dense foliage.

The two men they had lowered on the cable had already managed to enter the wreckage and assess the situation. When they had finished briefing the others, two of the men headed back the way they had come, following the slashed foliage to the chopper.

They returned with a black vinyl body bag, a folding wire mesh stretcher, and several pairs of black vinyl gloves. They also brought a pair of long handled hedge and tree trimmers.

Jamie smiled at the site of them. They looked like the ones Mr. Wilbert, the church custodian, had used to keep the forest at bay, to keep the grounds around the church and cemetery free of any unsightly growth.

After they had enlarged the opening in the side of the plane and the interior cleared of the invading vines and other growth, the body bag and the assembled wire mesh stretcher were exchanged for the tools that the men had used to clear the interior of the wreckage.

The others stood by, patiently waiting until the men inside returned to the opening in the side of the plane, carefully keeping the wire mesh stretcher level. The waiting men solemnly stepped forward and took it, like pallbearers, and gently removed it from the wreckage.

The glossy black vinyl body bag was stretched out in the stretcher, zipped shut over what appeared to be the gaunt remains of a body.

Jamie moved back in astonishment. He had been so obsessed with having his own body recovered that he hadn't given any thought to the fact that there could be others in his same predicament, or even worse.   At least his body had been taken in out of the weather.

He watched as the men carefully made their way through the slashed foliage back to the helicopter, loaded the stretcher into the chopper and secured it. Then four of them made their way back to the wreckage while the others waited by the idling plane.

The four men slowly circled the wreckage, one of them talking into a hand-held recorder as he went. Another one crawled inside the plane with a small camera. Jamie could see the flashes as the man moved around inside, taking pictures in all directions.

When the two men waiting outside the plane had finished they briefly checked their equipment and joined the one with the recorder and the other one from inside the plane, who had been making written notes of their own. The four of them appeared to gather for a short conference, nodding as they talked, calling attention to the faint marking on the plane's body and wings, then made their way back through the jungle to the chopper.

Jamie stayed above them as they approached the idling chopper. They gathered by the side door in the fuselage with the other men and appeared to be briefing them, sharing their observations and the general condition of the wrecked plane.

The pilot, who had unhooked his seat harness and turned to listen, nodded as they talked and gestured.

Then when their impromptu conference ended and they all began taking their places in the helicopter, buckling themselves in, the pilot turned back in his seat. He fastened his own seat harness and began to rev the engine, the rotors wash causing a whirlwind in the foliage and rotting ground cover.

Jamie watched the chopper rise slowly from the foliage, hover there for a moment, then swing around and tilt slightly as it headed off in the direction of where he had first seen it appear.

A wave of trepidation swept over Jamie as he watched the plane grow smaller. It was the same sensation he had felt the day he watched the other prisoners, and even the guards, disappear into the foliage, leaving him and his crumpled body to the mercy of the squalid jungle.

Chapter Twelve

Jamie couldn't help but feel a niggling anxiety as he watched the helicopter dwindle into a small dot and disappear over the horizon. He wanted to believe they would come back for the plane. Wanted to believe they knew about his body and would come back to the village.

He glanced down through the foliage to where the crumpled plane was swallowed up by the jungle growth, then began to move slowly, almost reluctantly, toward it. He hovered just above the wreckage, examining it carefully. He realized he knew nothing about planes and what could be considered salvageable, but the condition of this plane from not only the crash, but from time and the forces of nature, too, made him wonder.

There had to be something here that they would come back for. He moved along each side of the plane then slowly entered the fuselage. The inside looked even worse than the outside. The jungle had really taken over.

He could see the dark spots on the remains of the rotted body harness and the pilot's seat. He could see where they had cut the rotten belts and where they had cut the vines and small trees to remove the body. He studied the other growth coming through the floor that they had trampled as they moved back and forth, then noticed that the instrumentation had all been removed from the cockpit. There was nothing but glaring holes and broken windows in the empty hull. And that was all split and twisted.

There were no gauges, no dials, no wiring. Nothing. He didn't know if planes had foot pedals, like cars, but there were none of any kind. Just some odd shaped holes in the floor where foot controls could possibly have been, with vines and other vegetation growing up through them.

Jamie rose above the wreckage again and hovered there, a feeling of despair creeping in on him. The guy taking all the pictures inside the plane and the one outside talking into the recorder were hopefully confirming that there was enough of the plane left to come back for.

He couldn't remember seeing any plane parts in the village, no gauges or wiring anywhere. The natives would have no use for any of those things, and they wouldn't have ignored the pilot's body, either. They would not have left it unprotected and exposed to the weather like that.

The thought that the pilot's body, whoever he was, had been found and would be returned to his family, lifted Jamie's spirits. It just wasn't his turn yet, but the guys in the helicopter coming for the pilot did lend credence to Jamie's confidence in the Army. He would keep an eye on the plane wreckage, now that they knew where it was, just in case.

His concern for the downed pilot brought Jamie's attention back to the other prisoners, Rebel and GA in particular, that had been loaded on the old boat. He was concerned about them, too. The last he had seen of them, they were heading off down that muddy river with those different guards. They were the larger men in black uniforms, who weren't Oriental.

The thought of his fellow prisoners, especially his two friends, opened a bleak panorama beneath Jamie. It was still night but the bright moon illuminated the vast landscape. There were snow capped mountains in the distance with a lone set of railroad tracks traversing the barren countryside. The jaded rails ran past a group of corrugated metal buildings with a loading dock at one end. The ramshackle wooden dock was serviced by a short rail spur.

Two low-slung rail cars had been shunted onto the spur tracks, their open tops even with the flooring on the dock. Each car was partially loaded with what looked like white sand by the light of the moon's glow.

Behind the metal buildings, out in the open and well away from the railroad tracks, were four frame buildings resting on what looked like upended concrete blocks. They were surrounded by a high wire fence with spiraling razor wire along its top. There were no windows in any of the buildings, just a door at one end with a couple of concrete blocks for a step.

There was no sign of smoke rising from the small metal tubular chimney protruding from the roof of each of the buildings, despite an abundance of snow covering the ground. There was, however, a small column of smoke lazily rising from the chimney of the other building. A more substantial frame building that sat between the fenced compound and the corrugated buildings by the railroad. And it was lighted, too.

Jamie was still trying to rationalize what possibly could have brought his attention to a place like this when the front door in the heated building opened and a squad of guards stepped out into the splash of light on the small porch, their breath vaporizing in the brisk morning air.

They wore the black uniforms and knee-high black leather boots, the same as the men on the boat had worn, but also wore fur-collared greatcoats and black fur hats. There were no rifles or bayonets, but each man carried a side arm in a covered black leather holster, attached to a black web belt girded tightly around their waist, on the outside of their heavy coat. Also, each guard had an intimidating black wooden nightstick shoved through a shiny metal loop on their belt.

The men walked along in a group, sort of a loose formation, to the fenced compound, their breath and cigarette smoke vanishing quickly in the crisp morning air. The lead man opened the heavy lock on the gate and they entered the bleak compound. Two of them waited by the gate while the other four separated, each noisily entering one of the quiet barracks.

Jamie began to understand as prisoners began to emerge from the buildings, adjusting and pulling on what little clothing they had. Each one looked down as he carefully placed his foot on the wobbly concrete blocks and stepped to the frozen ground.

He recognized Rebel first, as gaunt as the man was, by the way he moved and marshalled the other prisoners, then GA, haggard and stooped, but still taller than anyone else, including the guards.

He was surprised to see that the prisoners wore no shackles or restraints of any kind as they emerged from their meager shelters, nor was there any belligerence or show of force or weapons among the guards. They merely watched the men form up, then followed along, dourly smoking their cigarettes. A few chose to leisurely twirl their shiny cudgels as the prisoners moved off in the direction of the darkened corrugated metal buildings by the railroad track.

By the time the last of the prisoners had disappeared through the door of the largest metal building, dawn had broken over the horizon and began to illuminate the frigid countryside.

Jamie was still not sure of what kind of camp this was, or where it was that the prisoners were being held, or even by whom.

He wasn't familiar with the cold, bleak countryside before him as he moved closer and hovered over the two railroad cars. In the faint daylight there was still a little bit of a shine to the white stuff in the cars, but it didn't look like sand. Didn't look like any sand he had ever seen.

It took a moment for Jamie to realize the stuff in the two cars was not white sand, but salt, and what he was looking at began to come together. American prisoners of war being held in a labor camp, being forced to work in a salt mine. And being held somewhere in a really cold country that didn't appear to be at war.

The absurdity of it frightened Jamie. Rebel and GA, as well as the others would be there until the war was over. Or even longer, he supposed, if no one knew where they were, especially if they had been reported Missing-In-Action.

A feeling of impotence surrounded Jamie as the scene before him began to fade. He was still in a quandary as he drifted back to the thatched burial hut. He had accepted the fact that he could do nothing for the other prisoners, but a concern for them still plagued him.

Chapter Thirteen

There was nothing going on in the native village, nothing that Jamie should be concerned about. He could see nothing that would feed his anxiety, but the growing sense of urgency managed to stay with him.

He had been aware that there was nothing he could do for Rebel and GA, or the other prisoners, while he watched them come out of the dark barracks and fall into formation for their march to the salt mine. Their situation was disturbing, but that couldn't be what was gnawing at him.

Jamie calmly watched the villagers go about their business while he struggled with his dilemma. His frustration brought back the acronym the instructor in the training camp used when one of the exercises or training sessions didn't go exactly as they should have. SNAFU. Situation Normal, All Fouled Up. Of course, some of the wise guys, some of those who felt obligated to flaunt their pretense of worldliness used another word starting with an F in the place of Fouled.

While he recalled the few loudmouths that had been in the training camp with him, the ones who never missed a chance to be impudent, a chance to be vulgar, the door in one of the thatched huts opened slowly and a young girl peeked out. She hesitated for a moment then stepped to the ground and stood there, looking cautiously around before she pulled the door shut behind her. She hesitated again briefly then crossed to where several women were busy at an outside work table, peeling and chopping vegetables and what looked like some kind of roots.

The way the girl timidly made her way across the compound, it dawned on him that she was the one the three soldiers had abused. The girl who was rescued by the guy with the tiger claw necklace interred over there by the far wall. The scene of the man materializing in front of the soldiers flashed before him, then faded away and Rosemary came into view.

She was in the new supermarket out there on the highway south of town, walking away from the check-out counter pushing a shopping cart. He watched her hesitate while the automatic doors swung open, then push her cart through and head across the parking lot to his pick-up.

He smiled at the sight of the truck, glad it was paid for and happy for her to have it, but he could see nothing here that might be the cause of his anxiety, either. Rosemary was a good driver as well as a cautious person, and there were no vehicles moving in the parking lot that he could see.

Jamie hovered along above her as she approached the passenger side of the truck. While she unlocked the door and opened it, then pulled her grocery cart closer, he noticed movement in the gaudily adorned pick-up that was parked a couple of spaces away, over in the next row.

His anxiety flared anew as he recognized the vehicle, and watched Orris Fergerson step out and close the door. The domineering man smirked as he hitched up his pants in the back, leaned down to the large outside chrome rearview mirror to run a comb fastidiously through his hair and admire his reflection, then put the comb away and turn from the mirror.

Orris was older than Jamie and Rosemary, somewhere in his middle thirties, and hadn't been drafted because of some kind of injury he had supposedly suffered a couple of years ago at the sawmill over in the next county where he had worked. The man was quick to tell you that he was retired on Workman's Compensation and unable to take up arms in defense of his country, but willing and able to perform his patriotic duty of looking after the women the soldier boys had left behind, married or not.

Orris moved up to the front of his truck to watch Rosemary for a moment, then his smirk changed into an ingratiating smile as he stepped out and swaggered across the lot toward where she was transferring her groceries from the cart to the cab of the truck.

Jamie stayed close while Rosemary finished loading her groceries, then when she closed the passenger door and turned to push the cart around the back of the truck, toward the cart park, he drifted along behind her.

Orris quickly changed course to intercept Rosemary when she returned the cart and headed back to her truck.

Jamie's possessiveness recoiled at the man's insolence. Rosemary didn't live in the same world of Orris Fergerson or his kind. She was such a dear person, and got along well with just about everybody, but she had never encountered, or had to deal with someone like this guy, especially under the present circumstances, and alone.

Jamie hovered close behind Rosemary as Orris caught up and fell in step beside her.

Rosemary stiffened but kept walking, eyes straight ahead as she quickened her step.

"Mornin, Miss Rosemary."

She continued to ignore him and kept moving, haughtily keeping her eyes on the truck.

He stayed beside her, his voice taking on more of a lilt now. "And how are you this fine mornin'?"

Rosemary's eyebrows lifted scornfully, unable to see how her wellbeing could possibly matter to the man when he didn't even know her.

Orris kept walking beside her, smiling jovially, as if they were actually having a civil conversation. "Any word on the McFarron boy?"

Rosemary winced at the question but managed to continue to ignore him as she guardedly lifted her keys from her purse. He had never known Jamie, or her either for that matter. She couldn't believe the man was really interested, and besides she didn't care for the man's boldness or the callous way he had referred to Jamie.

When Rosemary stopped at the driver's side of the truck and reached out with the key to unlock the door, Orris moved in quickly and took her hand. "Here, let me help you with that, sweet thing."

Before she could even start to struggle to draw her hand away from his grasp, a roiling mist began to materialize to her left and behind her, swirling angrily as it grew.

Orris sobered quickly at the sight, his smirk fading away. His face blanched as a wisp of cold vapor snaked out of the misty dervish and icily encircled his wrist. The startled man let go of her hand and drew back as the spinning fog slowed and receded, leaving a surly Private Jamie McFarron standing there before him in full battle dress. Camouflage fatigues, camouflage cover on his helmet, a canteen, ammo and other field gear hanging from his web belt, and his rifle held at the ready in front of him, a glinting bayonet affixed.

Rosemary frowned in confusion as Orris suddenly gasped and let go of her hand. Her brow tightened as he drew back, bouncing off the vehicle behind him, the front fender of her truck, then turned and scurried off across the parking lot toward his own truck, not once looking back.

The man's sudden panic, his strange behavior and hasty departure gave Rosemary a bit of a chill. An eeriness embraced her that brought Jamie to mind, and the quiet times that they had often shared, talking quietly as they sat in front of the big fireplace or on the porch. She had always enjoyed his stories, particularly the one about a soldier who had been killed in World War One and was still buried somewhere in Europe.

The two of them were sitting before the fireplace that night and Jamie was talking about his Grandpa Jordan's stories of the departed souls among us that hung around a loved one. That was when he told her about how a Mr. Hutchens, the guy that was buried somewhere over there in France, and how he had materialized behind his wife to frighten away the unscrupulous man from the bank.

She whirled around quickly but there was nothing there. The apparition had faded as soon as Orris drew back from her, then stumbled as he turned and hurried away.

Rosemary glanced anxiously around the parking lot, opened the door to look inside the truck, then stiffened for a second before she wilted against the end of the seat in the truck. Her composure deserted her as she slowly raised a white handkerchief to her eyes.

Her voice as soft as a whisper. "Oh Jamie. No-o-o."

Chapter Fourteen

Jamie hovered above her, hurt by his carelessness as he watched her slumped there all alone, half in the truck, sobbing so wretchedly, crying so heartbroken into the damp handkerchief. It hadn't occurred to him that she didn't know, that she wasn't aware of what had happened to him, but he couldn't just let Orris pester her like that. He didn't even want the man near her, and, for sure, didn't want him to put his lecherous hands on her.

And he couldn't fault the Army, either. They could only list him as MIA or POW, or maybe both. They wouldn't know for sure what had happened to him until they found his body.

He hovered closer until she finally raised up, dabbing at her eyes while she scooted into the truck, then just sat there behind the steering wheel, looking out across the parking lot at nothing in particular.

Jamie's anxiety had begun to build again when she finally broke her stare, wiggled into position and fumbled the seat belt in place. She glanced around slowly with puffy eyes, holding onto the steering wheel while she reached out and pulled the door shut.

She rolled the window all the way down, like it was a chore, then slumped back in the seat and just sat there, holding the wadded handkerchief in her lap. Jamie had begun to wonder about her again when she suddenly bolted upright and glanced warily down at the seat beside her, then began rearranging her purchases, moving some of them to the floor, as though making room for a passenger.

At the thought of the possibility of Jamie actually being in the truck with her, or at least where he could see her, she moved her purse to her lap and took out a tissue and a small compact. She began dabbing at her eyes then turned her head from side to side as she fluffed her hair.

Jamie smiled down at her as she worked, making sure he stayed behind and well above the little mirror, out of her line of sight. Grandpa Jordan had told him a few stories of departed souls appearing in a mirror, sometimes even while a person was using the mirror, and he certainly didn't want that to happen here.

Rosemary had always been so concerned with how she looked. At first, when they had started getting serious about each other, he had thought she might have a physical problem that required so much time in a rest room, but then began to realize it was just that she was a woman. He began to understand that women seemed to think it was a sin to pass by a mirror without using it, even if it was only to check how clean it was.

While he watched her he thought of moving into the truck beside her, riding along closer to her, but he wasn't going to take the slightest chance of frightening her again, especially while she was driving.

This was all so strange to him. He didn't have any trouble secretly watching the other prisoners, or the natives in the village, but that was different. He didn't have the same feelings for them.

As he hovered over the truck he began to rationalize that extreme anger must have been what it was that allowed Mr. Hutchens and the native with the tiger claw necklace to appear before the ones they were angry with. He supposed that was what caused him to appear before Orris Fergerson, but he couldn't be sure. If ones emotions governed something like that, then he couldn't be sure that he wouldn't inadvertently do something to frighten her while she was driving, so he would have to be content to hover along above the truck and see that she got home safely.

She finally put her compact away, dabbed at her eyes one more time, then glanced around the lot while she started the truck. When she was satisfied that her way was clear she backed out of the space and headed across the lot to the exit.

At the stop sign she glanced back to make sure there was still nothing at the spot where Orris Fergerson had accosted her, then waited for a car to pass before she pulled out onto the highway and headed home.

Jamie was still floating above the truck when she pulled into the yard and stopped. He stayed where he was while she gathered up her purchases and went into the house, then drifted above the house to watch her, not quite ready to turn his attention from her yet.

He made no move to follow her into the house. Momma was more than likely to be there, to be in the kitchen when Rosemary came in and put her groceries away. And Momma would have no way of knowing what had happened to him, either. She got along well with Rosemary, treated her like the daughter she had never had, and would surely have confided in Rosemary if she knew anything.

He would just have to be content to watch Momma from where he was. He didn't want to take a chance on inadvertently doing something that might frighten her. Momma had never accepted her father's theory about departed souls hanging around for some reason. She was very serious about her religion and would laugh at the idea, even though Grandpa insisted that the story about Mr. Hutchens was true.

She said she knew a few of the people that swore the story was true, then she would laugh and say that didn't mean anything because she had heard them swear about other things, too.

One time, when Jamie was still in grade school, he had asked her about something in a story Grandpa had told him. She just pooh-poohed the question and said that Grandpa sometimes ate too much supper, then dozed off in his chair and got a little heartburn. That would cause him to have a nightmare, then when he woke up he would pass the story off to us children.

But she loved her father and respected him. She always qualified her criticism of him by saying that his stories were a product of a creative memory and imagination, and that was not unusual for a man his age.

Jamie watched Momma glance curiously at Rosemary as she silently put the groceries away, then picked up her purse and headed upstairs to her room.

Momma's brow wrinkled when Rosemary left without speaking. She glanced after the girl for a moment, then quickly began wiping her hands on her apron and hurried after her.

Chapter Fifteen

Jamie stayed where he was, hovering above the house, as he watched Momma frown her concern for a moment, then drop what she was doing and follow Rosemary up to her room. He wasn't worried that Rosemary would mention Orris Fergerson to Momma. Wasn't worried that she would try to explain what she thought had happened back there in the parking lot.

Rosemary was not a gossip, or one to share her own personal problems with anyone, not even him at first. Besides, Rosemary was well aware of how Momma felt about her father's stories of departed souls hanging around.

And Momma wasn't one to pry, either, just quick to console a loved one whether she was really aware of what the problem was or not. And wasn't usually too far wrong, even when she didn't know for sure.

Rosemary had grabbed a fresh tissue from the box on the bedside stand when she came in the room, then flung herself across the bed, but the tears were all gone. She had nothing left but despair and a dull ache with each beat of her heart.

At the sound of footsteps on the stairs, she pulled herself up and was   sitting on the side of the bed when the faint knock came.

"Rosemary, honey. Are you all right?"

She took a deep breath and let it out, but her answer was still hardly above a whisper. "Yes, ma'am. I'm okay."

Momma waited a moment, and when there was nothing further, no sound of any kind, she leaned closer to the door, her voice still soft. "May I come in?"

Rosemary nodded as she dabbed at each eye, then raised her voice slightly. "Yes, ma'am."

Jamie made no attempt to get closer as he watched Momma push the door open, step through almost reverently and close it behind her. He felt a warm glow of contentment surround him as she moved hesitantly across the room and lowered herself gently onto the bed beside Rosemary.

Momma kept her eyes down, kept them on her own lap as she sat there, apparently at a loss for words, sharing the girl's obvious anguish. After a vexing moment, when the quietness finally seemed to reach a crescendo, Momma reached over and gently took Rosemary's hand in hers, clasping it to her bosom.

She nodded devoutly as she patted Rosemary's hand and spoke just above a whisper. "I know, honey. I know how you feel because I love him too, and miss him so very much."

Momma turned and took Rosemary in her arms, still speaking softly over the girl's shoulder. "I've prayed to God every night since he left. I ask Him to look after Jamie, wherever he is. And now that the war is over, I ask the Lord to send him back to us when his job over there is done."

Rosemary raised the tissue to her eyes as she began to sob softly at the optimistic words, at the sincerity of a mother's supplication. She didn't really understand what had frightened Orris Fergerson today, and she didn't want to believe what her intuition was telling her, either, but all she could think of was that man from World War I that Jamie had told her about; the one buried somewhere in Europe. And if it was Jamie that had scared that awful man away today, then it would mean that he's...

Her mind stopped abruptly, refusing to even acknowledge that dreadful word. She had never known Jamie's grandfather, so all those stories were just that, stories.

She turned slowly and put her arms around Jamie's mother, patting her on the back as she spoke softly. "I know you do. And I've been asking God to keep him safe, too. I love him and miss him so much."

Momma drew back and raised the lower edge of her apron to her eyes. "If Jamie could see us now he would fuss at us for being so silly. He wouldn't want us to be sad. He would want us to be happy, want us to take care of each other and be here for him when he comes home."

A slight chill ran up Rosemary's spine at the thought of the encounter in the parking lot today. She was so confused, but there was still the possibility that Jamie might be nearby, might actually be here in the room, could be here watching them.

She straightened up, dabbing at her eyes as she spoke. "I'm sorry, but it's been so long and we've had no word. I can't help but worry."

"Now, now." Momma pushed herself up from the side of the bed and turned. "They just said he was missing, and you know Jamie. He'll manage to find his way home, one way or the other when the time comes."

Rosemary nodded, her mind still seeing the way Orris

Fergerson dropped her hand and took off across the parking lot. She was so afraid that Jamie had already found his way home. She wasn't sure of what Momma meant by 'one way of the other', and wanted to believe that it was nothing more than just a figure of speech.

Rosemary tried to think of what could have possibly frightened someone like that. From what she had heard about the disgusting man, he was such a colossal braggart, always fighting, causing trouble, and had even been arrested a couple of times. She couldn't imagine, really, that just seeing Jamie could have scared such a man that bad.

Her eyebrows raised at the thought of the man seeing a specter materialize before him was really what scared him. A shiver ran up her back at the thought. That would certainly scare her, too, but Jamie would never do that to her. That was probably why she, herself, hadn't seen anything.

Rosemary's reverie was broken when Momma took her hand and helped her up from the bed. "Jamie wouldn't want us to be upset, wouldn't want us to worry." She patted Rosemary's hand again, then turned toward the door. "Come on, I had just taken some cinnamon rolls out of the oven when you came in. I'll put the coffee pot on and glaze them while it's perking, then we'll have a snack and talk about the good times, talk about what we're going to do when Jamie comes home."

Chapter Sixteen

Jamie watched them make their way quietly down the stairs, Momma walking cautiously sideways, one hand sliding along on the banister behind her and the other held out toward Rosemary, to steady the girl should it become necessary. But Rosemary was coping with the stairs very well, slowly regaining her composure even though she was still dabbing at her eyes as she followed along a couple of steps behind.

When they reached the kitchen Momma pulled a chair out from the table and settled Rosemary into it. She leaned down and put her arm around the girl's shoulder, gave her a fervent hug, then patted her on the shoulder affectionately and turned toward the cabinet.

Momma glanced back and forth, keeping her eye on Rosemary while she filled the chrome percolator and plugged it in, then set out a small mixing bowl with a spatula and the ingredients. She stood sideways to the cabinet, talking quietly while she mixed the glazing and smeared it on the pan of rolls that were waiting on the small wire cooling rack on the cabinet.

Jamie had drifted along as they left the bedroom and went down the stairs, his attention still on Momma's remark about the war being over.

If it was really over, and he had never had any reason to doubt Momma's word before, that could be why they had come looking for the plane and the pilot. Could be why the Army had started accounting for their POW"s and MIA's.

Jamie had no idea how long it would take for them to come back for his body, or even if they knew where it was, but he had confidence the Army would find a way, that they would eventually be along. He could understand there were many more than just him, but he was sure they would be here in due time.

His musings took him back to the frozen countryside with the shabby barracks and the corrugated metal buildings by the railroad track. While he watched, a lone figure struggling with a loaded wheelbarrow with salt piled high, came out of the building onto the dock. Jamie squinted as he watched the man cross the platform, upend the wheelbarrow into the low sided rail car alongside, then turn and make his way back across the dock, listlessly dragging the empty wheelbarrow behind him. It wasn't too difficult for Jamie to recognize GA, even as haggard and stooped as he was now.

Jamie had no idea how long the war had been over. Momma's remark hadn't mentioned that and he had lost all sense of time, so he had no concept, really, of how long Rebel and GA had been working here in this salt mine. But now, with the war over he was surprised to see that the prisoners were still being held here.

He tried to attribute their still being here to the fact that the place really did look isolated and the news just hadn't had time to reach such a remote operation yet.

While Jamie watched, trying to rationalize why the prisoners were still here, another figure just as haggard and bent as GA, came out of the building pushing a heavily loaded wheelbarrow. He dumped it into the railroad car, hesitated for a moment to lean on the upended wheelbarrow before he shuffled tiredly back across the platform, pulling the wheelbarrow behind him, and disappeared into the building.

Jamie was sure the man wasn't anyone he had ever seen before, but it did make him wonder how many other prisoners there were working here besides the ones from the camp he had been in.

He waited, watching the gaunt figures come and go across the old dock, hoping to maybe see GA again, and Rebel, too. Rebel had been a godsend to them back in that fetid prison camp. He had cajoled them, had gone out of his way to keep their spirits up, wouldn't let them give up hope even when he himself probably felt there was nothing left to hope for.

When Jamie began to realize that he had seen GA make several trips, and one or two of the others that he was sure had crossed the dock before, he became concerned with the absence of Rebel and began to surmise why he hadn't seen the man.

He tried to think it was because they had recognized that Rebel had a knack for keeping a group's spirits up, or that they could possibly have made him a foreman of sorts. Could have him down in the mine, overseeing the digging and shoveling, or whatever they had to do to get the salt loaded into the wheelbarrows. A person like Rebel could surely run the operation more efficiently than a bunch of egotistical guards with rifles, or billy clubs.

Rebel had detested the guards' hostility and wanton cruelty back in the POW camp, and repeatedly suggested to the guards that a man could be led a lot easier than he could be driven. But the people running the camp apparently had no one that understood him, had no one capable of leading or even interested in anything other than arrogance and brutality.

Jamie refused to even acknowledge the possibility that Rebel hadn't been able to do the required work with his crippled hands, hadn't been able to keep up and suffered the same fate that he himself had back there in the jungle. But he was aware that Rebel was not a novice. He had seen the way the man handled himself under the worst possible conditions.

And the people on that old boat, probably some of the same people guarding the operation here, were not so belligerent. Not so brutal and quick to abuse a prisoner as the Orientals were. There didn't appear to be any bayonets here, and some of the guards were only wearing a side arm. And besides, he thought, they apparently had a shortage of workers or they wouldn't be using prisoners of war.

As the scene below him changed to the POW camp by the larger river, the one with the weathered dock where the old boat had left from, Jamie began to realize the war might very well have been over for quite a while. The thatched buildings inside the bamboo fence were all in a state of disrepair, and the fence itself was on the ground overgrown by the vines weeds. Just a few of the posts were still standing, and they were nothing more now than a trellis for the encroaching vines.

Chapter Seventeen

Jamie mulled over his situation and the state of things now that the war was over. He had conceded somewhere along the way that he was no longer a part of the world, but his body was and he intended to make sure it was found and sent home. He understood the word closure much better now and felt that he owed it to his family, and certainly to Rosemary. The thought of upsetting her still rankled him, but he wouldn't hesitate to do it again should it became necessary.

While his thoughts wandered, the scene before him had changed to the small makeshift camp where he had been held right after he was captured. It appeared to have been abandoned some time ago.

The bamboo cages had disintegrated, their parts piled haphazardly where they had fallen when the vine bindings had rotted and released them. The whole camp was in a state of disarray, the buildings and wire fences, as well as everything else, had been taken over by the creeping jungle growth.

A tall, lush stand of bamboo and other jungle foliage had cropped up where the large outdoor latrine had been. He had never really seen much of the camp, just what he could see and smell from the cage, but there certainly wasn't much left now of whatever had been there.

Jamie was aware of how fast the jungle could claim something that had been abandoned, but even at that it would have taken a number of years of neglect, years without any form of human habitation for the prison camps to reach their present condition.

And, yes, he thought as the scene before him moved farther back on his short military itinerary, even the small Army Post where he had been assigned, and was operating out of when he was captured, was no longer thriving like it had been at the time he was stationed there.

The camp was apparently being maintained, but there was no sign of military activity of any kind, just a lone Army Jeep parked in the small lot at the side of the Administration Building. It was gratifying to see the American flag again, even with it hanging limply on the pole by the front entrance.

At the back of the mess hall a cook, in white pants, T-shirt, apron and chef's hat, with a cup of coffee and a cigarette, sat in the shade of the mess hall on a straight wooden chair. He had the chair tilted back against the building, and just sat there looking around at nothing in particular. He did glance around occasionally toward the two soldiers sitting outside the back door of the mess hall, who were working lackadaisically at something, possibly peeling potatoes. Jamie had already conceded that it did appear the war was really over and his attention drifted back to the burial hut in the jungle to wait for the Army to come for his body.

He was surprised to see the village women gathered at the open work table, busily wrapping a body. They had apparently started working at the feet, lifting the large fronds one at a time from the pile being replenished by the group of boys. The women had reached the upper part of the body before one of them stepped away for a moment and Jamie caught a glimpse of the white coat with the leopard skin edging.

The idea of the village Chief being gone was disturbing. Jamie was still trying to accept what he was looking at, trying to ponder who now would be there to show the Army people where his body was when he recognized the native who had been the Chief's assistant. The native who had waited by the tree to guard his body while the others went to get help stepped out of the Chief's large hut, and crossed slowly to where the women were working.

The apparent new chief was wearing a long striped coat and woven palmetto frond hat with a snakeskin band. The snake's head, jaws gaping to show its fangs, was positioned at the front of the hat, just above the brim. The man's coat was made up of wide vertical strips of some kind of coarse cloth; each strip dyed a vivid orange, brown or a light cream. A small pouch made of snakeskin, possibly from the same snake as his hat band, swung from his long bamboo staff on a thin cord of braided jungle vine.

Jamie hadn't really forgotten the man, but was glad to see him as possibly the new Chief, glad there was still someone here who knew about him. Someone in apparent authority, who could direct the Army people to where his body had been interred in the burial hut.

While the women were wrapping the body, a group of the men had been erecting a low stand to hold the bamboo stretcher containing the body, sort of an improvised bier.

When the women were finished they stepped back and the men reverently moved the cocooned body from the work table to the bamboo stand they had built in the middle of the open compound.

Jamie watched the natives meticulously stack the wood for several large bonfires around the compound, then don their funereal masks and other ceremonial raiment. As it got dark they lit the fires and began performing their sacred rituals, continuing throughout the evening and into the wee hours of the morning. The fires continued to burn brightly until dawn began to creep over the horizon, then they were allowed to burn down into just a pile of glowing embers.

The lavish ceremonies ended with the solemn moving of the body into the burial hut and placing it on a newly erected bamboo shelf on the far side of the large room.

The cocooned body was secured to their satisfaction, and the old Chief's woven thatched hat, with the gaping tiger's head on it, was placed in a position of prominence on the enshrouded body. When the interment ceremony had been completed they all stepped back and bowed their heads.

The elderly native in the long green coat and woven straw hat with the crown of thorns on it, the prominent figure in each of the previous rituals, stepped forward and went into a measured plainsong. He raised his ornately carved wooden staff to the heavens several times as he chanted, then finally began to wind down, using the wooden staff to cross himself with great abandon as he turned toward the door. The new Chief and the group of men all turned and solemnly followed the old man out of the hut.

Jamie remained in the large thatched mausoleum, hovering just above his own body. It had begun to occur to him that time was moving on. The old Chief was gone, the war was over and it was time for the Army to come and get his body.

Chapter Eighteen

Jamie moved into his usual position above the burial hut where he could keep an eye on his body, and also watch the sky and surrounding jungle. Particularly, the horizon in the direction where the helicopter appeared when it came for the pilot's body. And, too, any movement in the vast sea of foliage that an Army recovery unit on the ground might make.

With the quietness in the village, and the solitude of the burial hut, Jamie's attention returned to the plight of Rebel and GA, and the other prisoners that were still working in the salt mine. With the war ended, the people operating the salt mine would surely release the prisoners and send them home, or at least notify the Army where to find them.

The thought of Rebel's crippled hands and GA's gauntness disturbed him. The two men would need some attention before they could actually be discharged and sent home. GA's condition could possibly be corrected with rest and some decent food, if he hadn't been crippled in some way or contracted a disease along the way. That, too, could be healed because the Army had some of the best hospitals and doctors in the world.

Rebel's crippled hands and the fact that he hadn't seen the man in either of his two visits to the scene of the salt mine caused him to hesitate again. He refused to even entertain the thought of Rebel being gone or that his hands were beyond being fixed. The fingernails had surely begun to grow out again by now, but he wasn't sure about what the doctors might be able to do for Rebel's crushed thumb joint.

Jamie still thought about the way Rebel had ignored the guards that ill-fated morning back there where they had stopped overnight in the jungle. He would never forget how the man had ignored the guards' threats. How he stepped past them to reach out and put his bloodied hands under Jamie's armpit and lift him to his feet. The man had to have had some pain of his own, but he never flinched or made a sound.

The idea of Rebel and GA being released and returned, even though they would need a lot of medical attention and convalescence, made Jamie even more aware of his own situation. The other prisoners, too, would be returned to their homes and families, and eventually be able to put it all behind them and go on with their lives.

But his own failure at being a soldier had taken all of that from him. There would be no reunion with Momma and Poppa, or Jodie. He hesitated at the thought of how he had frightened Rosemary, and the fact that she would have to go through it all again when his body got back home, but he couldn't just hang there and let that bully put his hands on her.

There would be nothing for the Army to return but his wasted body, and in a closed casket, no doubt, but at least that much of him would be back home. There would be a funeral, then his body would be buried in the cemetery behind the church, to give his family and friends…

There was that word *closure* again. He intended to see that his family, and Rosemary had it, but he, himself, would never have it. He would never be able to accept the way he had failed them and his country.

He had never entertained the thought of being a returning hero, or doing anything out of the ordinary. He had just accepted the draft call and went to do his rightful duty.

The short time it took for his training, shipment overseas and going on his first patrol, flashed before him again. None of it had prepared him for that night he stepped in that hole. One of the enemy's many booby traps. Those kinds of things had been mentioned during training, and again when he arrived at the in-country camp overseas, but how was he supposed to spot something like that in the dark.

Jamie had reluctantly accepted the blame for what happened. They had been briefed that night before they left on patrol, and been given a signal to use in the event of an emergency, but the thought of having been bitten by some kind of jungle snake, and the training instructor's remark about that square needle had caused him to panic.

He hadn't thought about the signal, or even been able to treat his leg properly before he was stripped of everything and being jostled along through the jungle with his hands painfully bound in front of him with barbed wire. When he tried to call their attention to the fact that his leg needed attention, they just prodded him along with the butts of their rifles.

Jamie had no idea how long the war had been over, or even how long it had lasted, but now that it was over it was time for them to start looking, time for them to start accounting for those that were missing, time for them to come on out here and find his body.

He was grateful to the natives for rescuing his body from the jungle elements and interring it with their own people, with their important people, no less, but his body needed to be back with his own people. He couldn't give up until that had been done, then he would try to figure out what he was supposed to do from there.

Since he had managed to frighten Rosemary, he had experienced a terrible urge to check on her, but he didn't want to frighten her again. He had become more aware of the distant light since his blunder there in the parking lot. Since then he had experienced a gravitational urge toward the light more than once, but he couldn't do anything now but wait, wait for the helicopter or an Army recovery unit. He had already screwed up enough.

He couldn't help but cringe at the thought of his flag-draped casket being carried into the church by solemn pallbearers in their caps, from one of the veterans service organizations in town.

There would be Momma and Poppa and Jodie and Rosemary, as well as the good people of the church. They would be standing in their pews as the flag-draped casket moved down the aisle, standing to bestow an honor that he didn't deserve.

But he still wanted his body to go home. Wanted them to know why he hadn't returned when the war was over.

Chapter Nineteen

Time began to drag, becoming monotonous as Jamie waited. He fought the urge to check on Rebel and GA again, trying to convince himself that it would be a waste because they had probably already been released by now and would be on their way home.

And there was Rosemary. He tried to convince himself that he wasn't afraid to check on her, it was just that he didn't want to scare her again. But he had never been any good at deceiving himself.

He was sorely aware now that she knew what had happened to him, and enough time had probably elapsed for her to accept the fact that he wouldn't be coming back. And he had not been able to completely banish the thought that she might possibly have turned to someone else. The very idea distressed him, hung over him like an affliction.

The mere possibility did not set well with him; did not set well with him at all. He understood that he no longer had any right, if he ever had, to approve of what she did or who she saw, but his feelings for her had not died with his body. He wasn't sure if he could watch her being consoled by someone else, especially someone he didn't approve of, or even if he still had the right to be possessive or even protective. But he would still do his best to keep her from being taken in by some scoundrel, still do his best to protect her from the Orris Fergersons of the world.

He was afraid to check on Momma and Poppa, too. Momma had never commented on her father's belief in the spirit world or his insinuation that there were souls hanging around for some reason. When she happened to be within hearing distance of Grandpa Jordan while he was talking about the souls among us and why they were still here, she would just raise her eyebrows and look at him askance for a moment, then shrug her shoulder and go on with what she was doing.

Momma never even questioned Grandpa Jordan's interpretation of the scriptures and other sources he used in explaining his belief about the lost souls among us, but she never agreed with or encouraged him either.

Poppa, on the other hand, had listened to his father-in-law regale him, and anyone else who would listen, with stories of apparitions and avenging spirits. Grandpa often mentioned Oscar Hutchen's spectral appearance as proof when talking about his obsession with the concept.

Jamie had heard Poppa's version of the Hutchens story often enough as he grew up, but he had never decided whether it was because of Poppa's admiration for Mr. Hutchens, or his lack of respect for the man from the bank. And then there was Jodie. You never knew what that little scudder thought about anything, even when you heard him talking about it. Jamie's little brother had no qualms about talking to anybody, no matter who or where they were, or how long it had been since they had passed on.

Jamie still grinned when he thought about the time he and Jodie had been hunting all afternoon, and Jamie, ready to go home, turned in the direction of the last lone owl hoot he had gotten, so he could catch up with his little brother. He had stopped, though, when he heard Jodie's voice. It was low but extremely sincere.

His little brother was openly talking to Noah about the flood and the animals he had taken on his Ark. Apparently from Jodie's experiences with pet rabbits, he was telling Noah he could understand his taking two of each animal on his boat, and why, and then said he had never seen it mentioned anywhere in the Bible about how many rabbits there were on the Ark by the time the flood was over.

The teacher had even sent a note home with Jodie one time, telling Momma and Poppa that it wasn't in the boy's best interest to talk to himself like that all the time.

Poppa had cornered the teacher after church the next Sunday and explained that Jodie never talked to himself. Poppa made it abundantly clear that the teacher understood Jodie was active in Sunday School, and in Vacation Bible school every summer, where he had learned he could talk directly to God at anytime, and about anything. He explained that Jodie felt that if he could talk to the top Man, then he could also talk to anyone on down the line, no matter who or where they were.

Jamie's musings were interrupted by a sudden dot on the horizon in the direction of where the helicopter had appeared that had come for the pilot's body. He watched the dot as it grew into another helicopter, throbbing laboriously even though it was somewhat smaller than the other one. The plane seemed to be working the foliage, searching in some kind of pattern until it suddenly veered toward the site of the crashed plane and the small opening in the lush greenery where the other helicopter had landed.

He moved closer, watching the small plane circle the area slowly and come to a stop, then hover over the wreckage of the crashed plane for several minutes before it moved back to the small opening in the foliage and settled gently to the ground.

There were only three people, besides the pilot, in the small bubble of the chopper's body, all wearing camouflage fatigues. They stepped out cautiously, stooping to avoid the rotors as they gathered at the edge of the opening in the jungle. They talked back and forth, consulting maps and compasses, and marking their clipboards while the pilot worked at shutting the twirling blades down to an idle.

The pilot then unfastened his harness belts and shifted in his seat until he was more comfortable. He was apparently preparing to wait in the plane until the others had examined the wreckage for any identification that might still be there, and whatever else they could find.

Jamie watched the three soldiers talk and nod as they conferred, jovially horsing around as they continued to stretch, then turned and retrieved their back packs. They juggled them into place on their backs and tightened the straps, then picked up their clipboards and headed off through the jungle toward the wreckage of the crumpled plane.

The three soldiers occasionally stopped and glanced up and around as the series of measured single owl hoots echoed through the jungle. Even while they examined the wreckage and made notes on their clip boards, they continued to look for the source of the soft hoots in the trees above them, and as they made their way through the jungle back to the helicopter.

Chapter Twenty

The pilot turned around to face the front, fastening his seat harness while the three soldiers stowed their backpacks in the body of the chopper and strapped themselves in. After he had buckled himself in he began to sporadically rev the rotors, holding the throttle open longer each time. He continued to rev the motor until the rotors finally reached a piercing whine, then the small chopper began to rise from the jungle floor.

As the plane rose above the foliage the pilot looked up from the instruments and controls he had been manipulating and began to look around to get his bearings. He noticed the small, spinning wisp of grayish vapor hanging in the air a couple of feet out from the windshield, directly in front of him. He tried to ignore it, but couldn't seem to take his eyes from it.

It didn't appear to be coming from any part of the plane, or from the jungle below, and it was not being disturbed by the wash of the rotors.

He let the light craft hover where it was while he watched the small whiff of whatever it was that seemed to be concentrating on him, anticipating his next move. It was mesmerizing.

As the pilot put his hand on the control to veer off to the right, in the direction from where he had come, a soft lone owl hoot sounded in his ear phone and the little whiff of vapor, or whatever it was, began to pulsate as it slowly approached the bubble directly in front of him. It hung there for just a second, long enough to intrigue him, then moved off to his left and stopped, as though waiting.

The pilot nervously glanced up at the rear view mirror above him to check on the other three soldiers seated behind him. He wanted to see what their reactions were to the thing out there, but two of them were already asleep and the other one was bent forward, his upper body resting on his thighs, busy replacing the boot on his left foot.

Another soft owl hoot sounded in his ear phone, and the wisp of vapor, pulsating again, began to move cautiously off across the tangle of trees and vines below. The pilot unconsciously brought the chopper around and followed the small vibrant wraith across the vast canopy of foliage.

The pilot had already spotted the opening in the jungle foliage ahead, then as he approached he saw that it was occupied by a native village. He stopped at the edge of the clearing and hovered until he could spot the foreboding little wisp of vapor and try to understand what was going on, to understand what he was supposed to do.

The willowy wraith had crossed the open compound and was clearly visible as it hung just above the top of a large thatched hut on the far side of the village. The hut appeared to be more than just someone's home, more than the other ones there, and it was set back away from the other huts, with ample space in front for him to land.

As the pilot cautiously crossed the clearing a native in a multi-colored coat and a thatched hat with some kind of ornament on it came out of one of the huts. The man quickly took in the situation and began waving the curious natives back, away from the open space in front of the large hut, then stepped back out of the way himself.

Jamie stayed where he was while the pilot set the chopper gently down, idled the rotors, and the three soldiers finally stepped out. They glanced up at the top of the large hut, looking for whatever it was the pilot had told them about, then looked quickly around the village. After a moment they moved off toward the Chief who had stepped away from his own hut and started toward them.

After the ritual greeting, some arm waving and nodding, the Chief turned and ushered the three soldiers into his hut. It wasn't long before a native came out of the Chief's hut and hurried across the compound to fetch the Elder native in the green coat and thatched hat with the cross on it. Jamie recognized the man as the one who had officiated at the entombment of both his body and the body of their late Chief.

While the native ushered the Elder across the compound and into the Chief's hut, Jamie watched the Chief nod and raise his arm toward the burial hut as he conversed with the three soldiers.

After the Elder had taken a seat at the table with the Chief and the three soldiers, and given responsive nods to the Chief's and the soldiers queries, the five of them rose and filed out of the hut. The soldiers followed the Chief and the Elder as they crossed the compound and entered the large thatched burial hut.

Jamie watched the Chief and the Elder confer as they approached the shelf where his body rested, bow their heads for a brief moment, then turn to the three soldiers. After more arm waving and hand signing, the Chief turned and reached for the small thatched hat covering Rosemary's bracelet resting atop the cocooned body.

The Chief turned back to the soldiers and lifted the small thatched hat away to reveal Rosemary's bracelet on its little bamboo stand. The three soldiers' eyebrows shot up at the sight of the shiny gold trinket. They removed their caps in unison as they gathered closer around the Chief to examine it and try to make out the inscription.

After a moment the Elder stepped up to the foot of the wrapped body and began pulling at the leaves until he had bared the toe and part of the lacing on one of the body's Army boots.

One of the soldiers stepped closer to examine what he could see of the boot, then motioned toward the door while he gave instructions to one of the other soldiers. The soldier turned and hurried out of the hut toward the chopper, replacing his cap and motioning to the pilot to get on the radio as he crossed to the plane.

While the pilot talked on the radio, consulting back and forth with the soldier at the same time, Jamie moved in closer to the soldier in the burial hut to look at the bracelet. It appeared to have withstood its sojourn under the little thatched hat very well. Jamie hadn't exactly forgotten about it. With the bracelet safely accounted for under the little hat, his mind had been on other things, but he was glad now that the guy at the PX had engraved it for him before he left on patrol that night.

It was comforting to Jamie to watch the soldier take a handkerchief from his pocket, polish the bracelet for a moment then gently fold the linkage under the nameplate and wrap the bracelet in the soft cloth. The soldier carefully placed the wrapped bracelet in one of the upper pockets of his fatigue blouse and buttoned the flap. Jamie felt a warmness surround him at the thought that Rosemary just might get her bracelet yet.

Chapter Twenty-One

When the pilot finished talking on the radio he switched it off, spoke to the soldier beside the plane for a minute, then began to rev the rotors as the soldier turned away and crossed back to the burial hut.

The pilot lifted the small chopper into the air slowly, moving ahead discreetly until he had vacated the open space in front of the burial hut, then set the plane back on the ground and shut the rotors down completely. After he had completed his check list and made sure the radio had been secured, he moved back to one of the seats by the opening in the body of the plane. He made himself comfortable where he could see the burial hut door, and also the open sky to the north.

Jamie watched while the Chief and the Elder conferred with the three soldiers. The opening that had been made in the shrouding leaves to expose the Army boot had been left as it was, and four natives had been summoned to assist the three soldiers with the handling of the body.

The four natives and the Elder were left to guard the body and have it ready to be examined and possibly removed when the recovery vehicle, a larger helicopter, arrived. The Chief and the three soldiers returned to the Chief's hut, and after a short conference with much nodding and hand signing, the three soldiers returned to the chopper to join the pilot and help him keep the curious natives back from the plane.

The four natives and the Elder had remained in the burial hut. When everybody was gone they moved away from the body to settle themselves for the wait.

Jamie drifted down directly above his body and moved back and forth to make sure everything was in order. When he was satisfied he took up a vigil above the burial hut again where he could see the open sky and watch in the direction the planes always came from.

He had waited so long, and now all of a sudden it seemed as though things were moving too fast. He had never lost his confidence in the Army, but just wanted them to move a little slower. He was so glad they were finally going to come for his body, but he hadn't given any thought to how he would thank the natives for their kindness; thank them for rescuing his body from the jungle.

He felt sure he might possibly run into the original Chief when he finally got to where he was going, but the present Chief was the one who had waited by the tree to guard his body. The man had squatted there until the others came, then helped them take the body to their village and place it in the burial hut among their fallen leaders and respected elders.

Jamie had been so obsessed with his trust in the Army, and the idea of being returned to his beloved mountains someday that he had given no thought at all as to how he might go about thanking these people.

His thoughts turned to the little white steepled church, and cemetery, up there on the side of the mountain, where he would make sure his body was headed now. It was the foundation of his faith, which had never failed to comfort and guide him.

When his ordeal was finished and he got to where he was going he would make sure to talk to the Man up there about all the people who had helped him and his family, and especially about Rosemary. He was still ashamed of the way he had frightened her, and the way he had failed them, and his country. And now he was going to open up all the grief again by coming home this way. If there was just some way that his body could be quietly returned home and buried in the family plot behind the church.

Thoughts of Rebel and GA crowded in on him again. They probably felt the same way about returning home that he did.

He grew serious about their situation as he thought of them working in that salt mine all this time. He was afraid to drift back to the scene to check on them before he left to make sure his body was properly taken care of. He couldn't bear the thought of Rebel and GA still being there, being held there until they were worked to death and buried in an unmarked grave far from home. Or even worse, just tossed down one of the worked-out shafts in the salt mine, never to be heard from again. Their families and loved ones never knowing what happened to them, never having closure.

There was that word again. It had always sounded so ominous before when he heard it used, but it was even worse from where he was now. He needed it so desperately and he was trying his best to furnish it to his loved ones.

If only there was someway his body could be shipped home and quietly buried with a private graveside service, but knowing Momma and Poppa, and the people at home, that would never happen.

He was sure that Rosemary would be expecting him to be returned like this. She knew he had been killed since that day in the parking lot, but he still couldn't help but dread the tribulations ahead. Couldn't help but cringe at the thought of them having to watch the flag draped casket move down the aisle, of their having to sit there and share the shame of his failure.

Jamie hovered quietly above the burial hut, embroiled in resolving his quandary. He realized that nothing would ever be the same for him. Even when his body reached home, was returned to Momma and Poppa and Jodie, and of course, Rosemary, and was buried. He was well aware that he would never be a part of their world again.

He understood the teachings of the Bible and wasn't afraid of what was ahead for him, but the only close family that he had up there, if that was where he was going, was Grandpa Jordan and Grandma Olga. If they had a way of knowing how he died, would they still be glad to see him?

A speck appeared in the distance and began to grow larger for a moment before Jamie began to hear the faint throbbing of the rotors. He watched the pilot in the small chopper hurriedly move into his pilot seat and pick up the radio, glancing toward the incoming helicopter as he directed it to the open space in front of the burial hut.

The Chief stepped out of his hut and clapped his hands loudly to caution the natives to stay back as the Elder came to the door of the burial hut to look out. The pilot of the small chopper and the three soldiers stayed close to their plane as the shadow of the larger chopper caused the natives to draw back as it darkened the clearing.

The large helicopter circled slowly, then hovered as if

gauging the available space below. It finally descended carefully into the clearing to touch down in front of the burial hut. The swirling sand and debris settled as the large rotors wound down and stopped.

Chapter Twenty-Two

The native Chief, in his garish striped coat, crossed to the burial hut on the other side of where the plane had landed, and waited with the Elder while the three soldiers moved away from the small chopper. The group slowly approached the larger plane, solemnly watching those inside. They stopped by the side door of the chopper and waited for it to be opened.

Jamie's attention was everywhere. Mainly on the large olive drab whirlybird that had just landed, but he also felt that he was abandoning Rebel and GA. He wondered how he could ever thank the natives enough, and how the folks at home would feel about the arrival of his body.

While he watched the large copter's rotors wind down and stop, the side door opened and one soldier hopped spryly to the ground.

When Jamie realized the man wasn't wearing camouflage fatigues, but a dress uniform, he looked closer as the man approached the Chief and the Elder who had moved over by the door of the burial hut. It was an Army officer, with little metal clips on each side of his collar and on his cap, glinting as he moved. Jamie wasn't too sharp on that kind of stuff anymore but he did feel better by the fact that someone of authority had come.

Jamie watched as the officer gestured and conversed with the Chief and the Elder. When the three of them finally turned to enter the large thatched hut, Jamie returned to his place above the building. As the officer and the two village Officials went through the door, the three soldiers from the small chopper turned from where they had been waiting by the larger plane and followed them inside.

The three soldiers held back from where the trio had stopped in the aisle in front of the cocooned body when they realized the Chief was quietly talking and motioning with his hands. Jamie felt like he could almost decipher the Chief's signings as the man talked.

The Chief raised his arm to point in the direction of where they had found his body, then motioned from there to the compound outside where they had brought the body to prepare it for interment. After a few more words and gestures the Chief motioned from the open compound outside to the door of the hut then down the aisle and nodded to where the body was now.

The officer stepped up to the body, and with the help of the Chief and the Elder holding the leathery leaves back out of the way, closely examined the army boot. Then he moved up to the bit of camouflage tunic showing in the second opening that had been made in the shrouding leaves.

When the officer had finished and stepped back to the aisle with the Chief and the Elder, one of the three soldiers started toward the officer. He unbuttoned the flap on an upper pocket of his tunic as he walked.

Jamie still hadn't been able to distinguish any of the other soldiers from each other, but he did remember that this GI was the one who had Rosemary's bracelet. He hovered down closer as the soldier withdrew the folded handkerchief and motioned to the officer with it. Jamie didn't need to be close enough to hear what they were saying as he watched the soldier unfold the handkerchief and hold it out for the officer to see the bracelet.

The officer leaned down and scrutinized the bracelet, turning his head back and forth between the bracelet and the soldier as he questioned him. After a moment the officer reached out carefully, with thumb and forefinger, and lifted the bracelet from the handkerchief. He examined it slowly, turning it over to examine the back of the name plate after he had scrutinized the engraving on the front again, then placed it back on the handkerchief the soldier was still holding out to him.

The soldier began to nod as the officer talked, raising a finger for emphasis, then waited for the soldier to respond. The soldier began to nod his understanding of the officer's instructions and started folding the handkerchief around the bracelet again. The officer reached out and patted the soldier's shoulder as the man finished wrapping the bracelet and slipped it back into the upper pocket of his camouflage blouse.

As the officer turned and headed for the door, the Chief motioned to the four natives who had been waiting with the Elder. The three soldiers remained where they were while the Chief talked and motioned to the natives, indicating where they were to take their positions when the body was ready to be moved.

When the officer came out of the burial hut, motioning to those still in the large helicopter, four soldiers jumped down from the plane and turned to retrieve a slender open-mesh stretcher, molded to fit a prone body. One of the soldiers picked up the folded black vinyl body bag in the stretcher, shook it out briskly and began unzipping it at they followed the officer into the burial hut.

Jamie moved closer when the officer and the Chief began directing the four natives and the four soldiers to gently lift the cocooned body and place it in the black vinyl body bag. Then, when one soldier started to zip the bag up the Elder raised his hand as he solemnly stepped forward.

The officer, Chief and the soldiers removed their hats and joined the natives in bowing their heads as the Elder raised his scepter and his closed eyes to the sky. The man used the carved staff to accent his pleadings as he began to speak in a rhythmic monotone.

When the Elder finished he lowered his scepter and stepped back. Those with hats replaced them, then the natives stood by as the four soldiers closed the long bag over the body, cocooning leaves and all, and picked up the mesh stretcher and headed for the door.

Two of the natives hurried on ahead to open the door while the other two followed along behind the officer and the Chief.

When the stretcher, with its black vinyl body bag strapped securely in it, had been loaded into the large chopper and the four soldiers had it secured into place, the officer shook hands with the Chief and the Elder. He turned to be sure the three soldiers had entered the smaller chopper, that now had its rotors idling, then, satisfied everything was in order, climbed into the large helicopter and closed the door behind him.

Jamie drifted over and entered the closed body of the large helicopter and took up a position directly above the stretcher while the pilot began revving the rotors. He felt negligent in not being able to thank the natives, or do anything to help Rebel and GA. He was still dwelling on his failings as the large helicopter suddenly revved for a moment, then lifted off and turned in the direction it had come.

When Jamie suddenly realized that the GI with Rosemary's bracelet was in the other plane, he dropped down far enough to see out, and spot the small helicopter. It was following along casting its own shadow not too far behind their bigger one as the two planes throbbed along, skimming above the vast canopy of lush jungle foliage.

Jamie's apprehension began to eat at him again. He had waited so long for the Army to find his body and send it home, and now that it was on its way, he couldn't absolve his shame. Momma and Poppa and Jodie, and Rosemary, he was sure, would never know or care how he died, and probably not the Army, either, but he would never be able to forget his failing as a soldier.

Chapter Twenty-Three

Jamie was aware of the blurring green foliage passing so swiftly below them, but his attention was on both the smaller plane scudding along behind them and the large opening in the jungle they had just left. He still felt some kind of relationship, a sort of bond with the natives and their village.

When he could no longer make out the opening in the jungle, he kept his eye on the thin tail of smoke from their cooking fire rising lazily into the atmosphere until that, too, faded into the distance.

He reluctantly rose to the ceiling again, above the stretcher with its black bag containing his body to wait for whatever was next. He had lost all concept of time long ago and most of the ways of the world that he was no longer a part of, but he intended to stay with his body until it reached home and was turned over to his family.

As he hovered above the stretcher, his feeling of dereliction toward Rebel and GA was mixed with a fear of how his body would be received by the Army and the people at home who had known him. He was not a deserter or a coward, just a green recruit that had screwed up, and it saddened him greatly to think that his family and Rosemary might have to share the embarrassment of his failure.

The two choppers suddenly changed course, veering to the right to leave the canopy of jungle and head out over a body of open water.

He could see a wide sandy beach in the distance ahead, and as they drew nearer he could make out a large group of buildings on beyond the expanse of sand. There was a row of barracks, a mess hall, paved streets and parking lots with an array of Army vehicles, jeeps and olive drab four door sedans scattered among them. But most of all he was glad to see the Stars and Stripes in all its glory, despite the coming twilight and the lack of breeze that let the flag hang limply on its metal pole in front the larger of the buildings in the compound.

The planes began to slow as they passed over the first of the buildings and turned to the left. The smaller plane slowed and hovered as the larger one approached a paved open space with a large black and white circle painted on it. The landing pads were behind a stuccoed two-story building with a large Red Cross on a white background over the front door, and painted on its roof.

When the larger plane approached the designated landing spot, the lights came on as the pilot carefully settled it down and idled the rotors for a moment before shutting them down completely. The smaller plane, which had been waiting back out of the way, then flew across to another black and white circle already lighted, closer to the building, settled onto the center of it and shut down its rotors also.

Jamie stayed where he was while everybody but the pilot unfastened their seat harness like tired travelers, then opened the door and stepped down to the ground. They waited by the plane while the soldiers from the smaller plane walked over to join them.

The group milled around by the large chopper, talking and gesturing for a few moments until four GI's in white pants and T-shirts, accompanied by an older man in a knee-length white coat, and carrying a clip-board, came out of the swinging double doors that opened onto the dock. They hurried down the ramp, one GI pushing and one GI pulling a gurney large enough to accommodate the open-mesh stretcher and its cargo waiting in the plane.

When the stretcher had been transferred from the plane to the gurney, the man in the white coat stepped up and began to question the officer from the plane. After several shrugs and much shaking of the officer's head, the man in the white coat stepped back and motioned toward the building and the double doors.

No one seemed to notice the small wisp of vapor hovering above the stretcher as the four medics solemnly moved the gurney up the ramp, across the dock and into the building. The man in the white coat and the officer from the plane followed along, chatting, nodding and gesturing without looking up as they walked.

The hallway, with its polished vinyl floor and white walls gave Jamie the impression of a hospital, but there were no patient rooms. Just doors on each side, all closed, until the procession stopped at one, opened it and moved the gurney inside.

It reminded Jamie of one of the small cubicles in the emergency ward of the hospital at home. Like the one where they had taken Jodie one time when he fell out of the barn loft and hurt his crippled foot.

The four medics made sure the brakes on the gurney were set, the stretcher was secure on the gurney, then nodded to the man in the white coat and the officer and left the room. After another few minutes of discussion, the officer and the man in the white coat moved over to the door. They continued to talk while the man in the white coat turned out the lights and pulled the door shut after they had stepped out into the quiet hall. They made their way along the dimly lit corridor, still talking as they approached the service desk in the small rotunda at the confluence of the many hallways.

Jamie stayed in the room, hanging above the stretcher, to wait for someone to come back and start checking his body.

After a while, when no one showed up, he began to think about checking on the people, particularly the four medics and the man in the long white coat. There was nothing he could do to direct them to the dog-tag under the heel of his left shoe, but he was anxious for them to find out who he was and start making arrangements to send his body home.

He was sure they had ways to identify a body like his, even if they didn't find the dog tag, and they would surely have to remove the leaves, whatever they were, before they could examine the body closer. Then they would need to clean the body up some even though they would put it in a closed casket for the trip home.

When things continued to remain quiet, when no one came back to the room, he drifted out into the corridor, and the building in general to look around. The helicopters had both been shut down with just a security light on each landing pad. The soldiers from both choppers, except the one with Rosemary's bracelet, were in a recreation room shooting pool and watching a small cabinet with a lighted screen in its front.

Jamie finally managed to locate the missing soldier, the one with Rosemary's bracelet. He was in a front office, a rather nice one, holding the bracelet out as he explained it to the officer there, then lifted it from the open handkerchief and placed it on the officer's desk. The officer wrote a note, picked up the bracelet and examined it closer for a moment, then placed it and the note in a clear plastic baggie and closed it by sliding the little tab across the top.

The medical personnel had all apparently finished their shift and left for the day, so Jamie drifted back to the room where they had left his body for the night, trying to understand their apparent lack of interest.

In his bewildered confusion Jamie remembered Momma consoling Rosemary up there in his room that day, telling her that the war had been over for a while. He began to realize that he was looking at the peace time Army, but he couldn't help but be a little miffed.

There were no limited daytime hours in a war zone, and he had been well aware that he was in a hostile area that night. He had admitted long ago that he, himself, had screwed up, but he couldn't perish the thought now that these people, peace time military, who operated on an 8 to 5 schedule, probably wouldn't have fared any better out there in the jungle that night than he did.

His resentment began to fade as he remembered the war was over, and he hoped these peace time soldiers would never have to worry about stepping into a hidden pit with poisoned bamboo stakes in it.

Chapter Twenty-Four

The large camp appeared to be coming to life, even before the approach of dawn, and Jamie rose higher so he could watch the rows of barracks and the administrative buildings as their lights began to come on. When there was no movement, though, no signs of anybody being out and about yet, he moved over to the nearest barracks, drifted inside and waited in a corner just below the ceiling.

He had been alone and away from the Army, away from the chaos of barracks life for so long that he had forgotten what a GI morning was like. When he was there he had never had time to even wonder what a barracks might look like in the morning. He was too busy competing for a commode or urinal, a mirror and sink to shave, some space in one of the open showers, and finally, just a little elbow room while he got dressed.

About half of the men were making their beds, laying out items of clothing, giving their shoes a quick swipe with a small brush or the corner of someone else's bedclothes, apparently waiting for one of the other men to finish and leave some space in one of the showers. He hadn't been in the Army long enough to become familiar with the word, latrine.

The other half of them were either shaving, splashing around in the shower or sitting on a commode yawning and scratching. A few of those had even let their head slump forward, back in the arms of Morpheus.

As the men finished their morning routines and got dressed they left the barracks a few at a time, hurrying across the compound to fall in at the end of the line going into the mess hall.

Jamie rose to where he could watch both the barracks and the mess hall. Soldiers were coming from all of the barracks now, creating quite a line at the mess hall. It was large but still the only one that he could see.

It had never occurred to him the amount of time and effort that it took to maintain an earthly body. And despite your best efforts in feeding and maintaining that body, you were still so restricted in your movements.

As he watched the camp continue to come to life, he realized that when he was still there, before he had been taken prisoner, before life was so abruptly taken from him, he was one of them, just another body in the crowd.

Like the burly sergeant in the training camp had said when he introduced himself and welcomed new recruits to the camp. "You're not a human being anymore; you're just a dogface soldier. Just another face and ass in a uniform."

Jamie's attention moved back to the small room where his body waited. The lights were still turned on in the room but there were no signs that anyone had been there yet this morning.

The black body bag was still zipped shut and didn't appear to have been disturbed during the night so he drifted to the ceiling above the stretcher and settled down to wait. He wasn't sure what the peace-time Army's hours were, or whether it was a holiday or week-end. He had just about forgotten all the discipline of an earthly existence.

He rose higher to take in more territory when he sensed someone in the hall. It was the man in the white coat, and an officer with a briefcase. He squinted down at the man to make sure he was the same officer that was on the large chopper when it came for his body.

They turned and entered the room, still talking as they closed the door behind them. The man in the white coat, the same one from yesterday, pulled the chair out from behind the desk and settled himself while the officer pulled a round-seated stool over in front of the desk with his foot. He straddled the stool precariously and leaned down to remove some papers from his briefcase, then scooted up to the front of the desk and rested his elbows on the edge.

The man in the white coat pulled a blank form from underneath the other papers on his clipboard and positioned it on top, under the clip, then smoothed it out with his hand. When the officer began to talk, referring to his papers as he nodded and gestured with his free hand, the man at the desk took a pen from the breast pocket of his white coat, leaned down over the desk and began to write.

Jamie caught enough of the conversation to know that the officer was telling the man what he knew about the body. Probably what the native Chief in the striped coat had told him back at the village.

After much nodding, gesturing and writing on the clipboard, the man placed it to the side, returned the pen to the breast pocket of his white coat and pushed himself up from the desk. The officer stood and returned the stool to where he had found it by the wall as the other man reached over and took a pair of pale rubber gloves from a box affixed to the wall.

They continued to talk while the man put the gloves on, pressing between the fingers until they were snug, then moved over to the stretcher and began to unzip the body bag. The officer moved over to the door and pulled it open, touched the bill of his cap briefly with a two-fingered salute, then stepped out into the hall and pulled the door closed behind him.

Jamie watched the man while he carefully unzipped the body bag, then just stood there looking at the two openings in the large leaves that were now as brown as cured tobacco. He was still scrutinizing what he could see of the shoe and the camouflage fatigues when another officer, an older man with a different kind of shiny emblems on his shirt collar, pushed the door open. He removed his cap and tucked it under his left arm as he solemnly stepped into the room and pushed the door shut, then quietly crossed to where the man in the white coat was still studying the two openings in the leaves.

After a short conversation the man in the white coat began zipping the body bag closed as the officer stepped over to the door. The man carefully replaced his cap, took a second to position it properly on his head, then pulled the door open and left.

Jamie watched the man in the white coat close the body bag all the way. He then removed the rubber gloves and dropped them into a waste basket, and went over to his desk and sat down to make some entries on his clip board. When he had finished writing, he picked up the phone, dialed, then leaned back in his chair to wait for someone to answer.

While the man talked on the phone, two orderlies, in white pants, T-shirt and short coats came in. They just nodded to the man on the phone, then walked over to the gurney bearing the stretcher and made themselves comfortable to wait for the man to finish his conversation.

When he hung up the phone the man began motioning and instructing the two orderlies as he stepped over and opened the door. He continued to talk and gesture as the two orderlies moved the gurney out into the hall. With a final word he nodded and went back into the room and the two orderlies moved off down the hall with the gurney, headed back the way the body had been brought into the building the previous evening.

Jamie followed along as they approached the same large helicopter that had brought his body this far. He hovered above as the two orderlies loaded the stretcher with his body, made sure it was secure, then hopped down from the plane. They turned and saluted the officer waiting in the plane, then stepped back as the side door of the chopper was closed.

When the idling rotors began to rev up, reaching a piercing whine, Jamie settled himself above the body bag. The heavy chopper shuddered briefly as it slowly rose from the pad, hung there for a moment, then tilted as it swung around and headed toward the airport at the large military facility that Jamie could sense off to the north.

Chapter Twenty-Five

Jamie remained in place above the stretcher, next to the concave ceiling of the chopper's body as he watched the blurring world pass below. An agonizing doubt rode heavy with him as he watched the world he had become familiar with fade into the distance and the world he had known before all sprawled out ahead, closing in on him much too fast.

He wasn't sure anymore if he was doing the right thing. He was well aware that there was no longer a place for him in the world that he had been gone from for so long, but there was still a place for his body. And he was sure that Momma and Poppa, and Rosemary, would want his body returned so it could be buried in the family plot, put to rest in its proper place. And Jodie? He was sure his little brother would never give up, would never be satisfied until that had been accomplished.

Jodie had never been known to say goodbye to anyone, especially family. He had told Jamie when he was heading back to camp, after his short after-training leave, that he would be right here if Jamie should need him for anything, then told him to take care, like he had always done before when Jamie went anywhere without him. And he had made it abundantly clear that he would still be right there when Jamie came back home. He had assured Jamie that he would be ready to help him build his house, the chicken coop and might even work on clearing some ground for Rosemary's vegetable garden while Jamie was gone.

The change in the pitch of the rotors, and the slowing of the plane's velocity broke Jamie's musing. He glanced around as they slowly approached the round black and white circle painted on the tarmac, off in a corner of the large airport. The pilot moved in cautiously, hovered to position the plane over the landing site, then set it down gently in the middle of the large circle. He cut the rotors back to an idle for a moment, then revved them one time and shut them down completely.

Jamie was aware of the large twin-engine plane moving slowly toward them as he watched the officer hop down from the helicopter and greet the approaching officer and the four orderlies that were pushing a low metal gurney to transfer the stretcher with its body bag.

The pilot of the large plane stopped it nearby and slowly pivoted it around on its left wheel until the plane faced the way it had come, then shut down both motors and the propellers feathered to a stop. The plane sat quietly where it had stopped, the only action a whirring sound as a long section of the underbelly lowered from the rear to provide a loading ramp into the body of the plane.

While the four orderlies pushed the gurney bearing the stretcher across the tarmac and up the ramp, Jamie moved into the interior of the plane to watch the loading, to see where they were going to stow his body. He wasn't particularly pleased with the idea of his body being relegated to the cargo hold, but when he got inside he saw there was just the one large compartment. There were two short rows of regular high-backed recliner seats on one side and several fold down shelves along the other side, equipped with straps for restraining stretchers.

When the four orderlies, and the two soldiers waiting in the plane, had transferred the stretcher and strapped it into place on one of the shelves, the four orderlies turned and headed back to the ramp with their gurney.

Jamie hadn't noticed before that the two soldiers who had been waiting in the plane wore dress uniforms, with a braided rope-like loop at their left shoulder and knee-high canvas leggings. Also, each of them wore a holstered side arm hanging from the wide webbed belt at their waist.

He drew back to the area above the stretcher and watched the two guards as they carefully went over the stretcher's moorings then took the seats at each end of the row nearest the shelf bearing the stretcher, and settled down as though expecting to wait.

Jamie was aware of the military's use of honor guards, but he had never associated any kind of honor with what had happened to him. It would be okay, he guessed, to have guards for his body while it was still in the custody of the Army, if that was what they wanted, but he hoped they wouldn't insist on any Honor Guards accompanying his body all the way home. He did not, in any flight of imagination, consider himself a returning hero. He was just another guy who had answered the draft call, fell to the enemy through his own blunder, and wanted his body returned and buried with his family. He realized it was a stretch, a lot to hope for, and maybe even have Rosemary buried beside him, when her time came.

The thought of Rosemary in his truck in the parking

lot that day still bothered him. He hadn't meant to frighten her, but he couldn't just stand by and watch that no-account Fergerson put his hands on her. He hadn't tried to check on her since that day, when she got home and Momma went up to her room, trying to comfort her after he had frightened her like that; after he had managed to foul things up so bad.

He wasn't real sure of what to think about Rosemary anymore, even though she was on his mind constantly. He realized that their earthly relationship had ended back there in the jungle, but he was hoping that she still lived with Momma and Poppa, hoping that she was still being considered part of the family.

And he was sure she would agree with Momma and Poppa to just have a private ceremony, if any at all, at the cemetery.

It would be nice for Rosemary to show up. He was sure that she would, but he had conceded long ago that she knew after that day in the parking lot that he was gone, and would understand that she was free to go on with her own life. He still hoped though that the return of his body would not be an embarrassment to her, or his family either.

The whirring sound of the loading ramp closing started a moment before he saw the officer that had been accompanying his body all the way from the native village. The man had a small suitcase in one hand and his briefcase in the other as he nodded to the two guards, then placed his suitcase in the small storage cabinet at the front of the compartment.

The officer turned and patted the shoulder of the guard sitting across from the head of the shelf bearing the stretcher, then moved down a couple of seats behind the man and sat down. He made himself comfortable, then opened his briefcase on his lap and took a folder out and began to read.

When the loading ramp had closed, the pilot started the engines, revved them for a long moment, then released the brakes and began to taxi toward the main runway.

Jamie glanced around, checking each person on the plane as it started to taxi into position on the runway for takeoff. There was the pilot, co-pilot, the officer, the two guards and his body. It was apparently a special flight to deliver his body to the next stop on its journey home, even though no one had made any effort to identify it yet.

How would they know where to take the body if they didn't have any idea whose body it was. His confidence in the army was beginning to fray a little, even though he realized he was not familiar with things like this.

He had been made to understand that concealing a dog-tag in your shoe was standard practice with prisoners of war, but he had gotten it from another prisoner, not through any training by the Army. He hoped the peace-time military people where they were going knew about the prisoners of wars little secrets.

His apprehension of the present day Army grew with the roar of the engines as the plane moved out, rumbling down the runway gaining the necessary speed to lift into the air.

Chapter Twenty Six

It was dark by the time the plane headed out over the vast ocean, its motors settling down now to a steady drone. The two Honor Guards had already put away their reading material and turned out their overhead lights. They both visually checked the stretcher, glanced around to nod to the officer, a silent good night, then put their seats back and closed their eyes.

Jamie's qualms had not waned as he watched the two guards lay back in their seats and close their eyes, right there in front of the officer, even though they had acknowledged his presence first. Then, after a long moment the officer closed his briefcase, put it on the floor under his seat, kicked back and closed his eyes, too.

None of the officers Jamie had run into in his short time in the Army would have allowed such behavior, especially the noncommissioned ones in the training camp. After revelry you were expected to be up and at'em all day, even when there was a short rest stop on one of the long hikes. He realized he wasn't too familiar with the workings of the peace time army, but this plane was carrying his body, and it was way out over a deep, dark ocean with nobody awake in the plane but the pilot and co-pilot.

There was no one else in the plane that he was aware of as he drifted   forward and entered the cabin. The co-pilot was slumped down in his seat, head back on the padded rest, eyes closed and his mouth open. Catching flies, as Grandpa Jordan used to call it.

The pilot was at least awake, but he appeared to be oblivious to the needles and lights on the dashboard, if that's what they called it. The man was casually thumbing through a magazine, not once looking up in the direction of the controls before him or checking the weather outside the plane, or even noticing whether the co-pilot was still alive.

Jamie was not familiar enough with planes to know about such things as an automatic pilot, but he didn't like what he saw.

At the sound of one low owl hoot in the close confines of the cabin the pilot slowly looked up from his magazine, squinting as he turned his head back and forth warily, listening.

When the pilot finally shrugged and dropped his eyes back to the golf magazine, the second hoot sounded, still soft but seemingly closer.

The man looked up guardedly again and slowly checked the entire cabin, then, as if it were a last resort, reached over and jabbed the co-pilot on the shoulder. All Jamie could see now was that both the pilot and co-pilot were ignoring the controls and the dark slanted windshield with the dash lights reflected so eerily in it before them.

With what appeared to be a scathing harangue by the pilot, and the fact that both men were now at least awake,

Jamie moved back in the plane, far enough to not have to listen to what was being said.

The co-pilot nodded respectfully, glancing around the cabin as he listened. Then began straightening his jacket and adjusting his cap as he carefully checked the controls before him.

When the pilot's harangue finally wound down and he went back to his magazine, and in the absence of finding anything amiss, the co-pilot settled back in his seat. He continued to periodically cast his bloodshot eyes over at the huffing pilot, still not sure of what caused the man's pique.

Jamie stayed where he was, unconcerned with what the two men thought about being interrupted like that. Jamie had already made one mistake, a huge mistake that night in the jungle, and he didn't intend to have to cope with another one, especially one of someone else's doings.

He was losing some of the confidence he had in the Army, the peace time Army, not the one he had known. He would watch these people as close as he needed to until they got his body safely back home. He would stay alert, watch everybody on this plane, at least until the plane got to wherever it was that it was going.

When he got back to the main compartment and the stretcher with his body, he found that the two honor guards were awake and checking the stretcher and the officer was up, too. The man was walking back and forth, watching the two guards as well as leaning down now and then to check the sky and the weather through the side windows. As dawn broke over the distant horizon ahead, the interior of the plane brightened slowly, chasing away the gloom and Jamie's restiveness.

Jamie felt the plane's thrust slack off slightly, and watched as the pilot began to circle over a rather large island below. He could see the huge airport and its buildings, and the American flag fluttering lazily on its pole. Off to the left was a high rocky cliff, with the rolling waves breaking onto the white sandy beach below.

What appeared to be part of a man-of-war vessel, just the bridge of a large Navy ship, was protruding from the center of the placid water of the bay. There was some sort of white structure built alongside the ship's superstructure. It looked like it might be concrete.

The troop ship carrying Jamie's company and others going over had only stopped for two days, giving them a chance to see the islands. Jamie had seen enough of Hawaii for him to realize where they were, but he didn't remember seeing anything that looked like what's out there now.

As the plane finally circled to approach the long runway, Jamie saw the long white vehicle, an ambulance with a bright red cross painted on its roof parked by the building at the head of the runway. An Army jeep was parked in front of the ambulance, headed in the same direction, as though it would take the lead, like it was ready to escort the vehicle to wherever it might be going.

A soldier sat placidly in the driver's seat of the topless jeep, watching the plane circle and come in for a landing.

As the plane straightened and lined up with the runway Jamie noticed that the two Honor Guards and the officer had returned to their seats and buckled themselves in.

When the plane had touched down and taxied up to the building, the pilot swung the big plane around with its tail toward the ambulance and shut down its engines. The whir of the long rear ramp began even before the propellers had feathered and stopped, lowering it slowly to the tarmac.

Two medical corpsmen had gotten out of the

ambulance and walked toward the back while the plane landed and taxied into place. They removed a gurney from the back of the ambulance and pushed it up the ramp where they were greeted by the officer and the two Honor Guards.

Jamie hovered above the stretcher while the two corpsmen worked at unfastening it and transferring it to their gurney, then turned to the back of the plane and came down the ramp accompanied by the two Honor Guards and the officer.

A solemn air surrounded the entire operation. There was no talking or even greetings by the participants, while the body was unloaded from the plane and placed in the ambulance.

The two Honor Guards stayed with the stretcher until it had been loaded, until the two medical corpsmen had secured the gurney in the ambulance, closed the rear door and got back into their vehicle.

Then the two Honor Guards hurried over and got in the back of the jeep where the officer and the driver waited. When they were settled and the driver had answered his phone and hung it back on the dash, the jeep pulled away slowly and the ambulance moved in behind it. There were no sirens or flashing lights as the motorcade left the airport proper, entered a city street and moved briskly along through the yielding traffic.

The small wisp of whirling vapor that rose through the roof of the ambulance and hovered above the top edge of the windshield was hardly noticeable in the busy traffic.

Chapter Twenty-Seven

Jamie wasn't familiar with the large city where they had landed, even though he had probably been here briefly years ago, so he had no idea of their destination until the driver slowed and followed the jeep into the gated entrance to an Army Base. As the jeep slowly approached the arm, a yellow and black striped barrier, the Sentry stepped out of his guardhouse. When the man saw the ambulance he raised the arm and came quickly to attention and saluted, stiffly holding it until both vehicles had passed.

The Jeep carrying the officer and two Honor Guards wound slowly through the streets of the huge Military Base, leading the ambulance until they approached one of the buildings in the Base Medical Complex. They circled around to the emergency entrance at the back, the Jeep slowing as it veered to the left and turned into a parking space across from the ramp leading up to the emergency entrance.

The officer and two Honor Guards got out and just

stood there by the Jeep, watching while the ambulance negotiated the sharp turn and drove up the ramp and stopped with its rear end adjacent to the double doors.

Jamie floated to the back of the ambulance and waited for the two orderlies to open the rear door. He kept his attention on them and the stretcher as they unfastened the gurney and carefully pulled it out.

The orderlies waited while the two Honor Guards and the officer crossed the lot and came up the ramp, then turned with the gurney and entered the building with an Honor Guard on each side. The Guards each walked with a hand on the gurney, assisting the orderlies as they followed the officer inside and stopped at a receiving desk setting in the center of a small rotunda at the confluence of the building's hallways.

The Sergeant at the desk rose and greeted the approaching officer while the two Honor Guards stepped over and shook hands with the lone Sentry stationed by the wall. The Sentry slid the strap of his rifle over his shoulder to be able to shake hands with each of them, then stepped back and brought his rifle into position again.

Jamie had risen high enough to take it all in. This peace time Army had him worried. They appeared to know what they were doing, seemed to be efficient enough, but nobody yet knew whose body it was, or even seemed to care, so how were they going to know where to take his body if they didn't know who it was. And they were so casual about it all.

He had never known a Sentry to shake hands with anybody while they were on duty, and nobody had made any attempt to salute anybody. In war time you saluted everybody to stay out of trouble, but these peace time soldiers hadn't made any effort to salute anybody. They were courteous enough, and respectful, but they just didn't salute.

He was aware that enlisted personnel never saluted each other but it had been made abundantly clear to him in training camp years ago that you wouldn't dare pass an officer without saluting.

He didn't get the idea that any of these soldiers or officers actually knew each other, the hand shaking was just a formality, but no one had as yet paid any attention to who his body was, or made any actual effort to identify it. He just hung there, watching the people until another officer came down the hall and approached the Sergeant at the desk.

They talked quietly for a moment before the officer from the plane joined them. He talked to them at the desk for several minutes, and passed some papers to them from his briefcase. The newly arrived officer scanned the pages for a minute, then threw a quick two-fingered half-salute, shook hands with the officer and the two Honor Guards and raised his hand in a farewell gesture. The three of them turned and headed back the way they had come, returning to the Jeep and the airport.

The gurney with his body was still parked next to the wall with only the one sentry, the newly arrived officer and the Sergeant at the desk. Jamie was sure they had more to do than just wait here with his body, but he was becoming concerned with their dawdling.

He realized the Sergeant at the desk had made several phone calls, on instructions from the remaining officer, but Jamie still felt they could do better than this. He had never had any personal contact with officers in his short Army career. His Company Commander in the training camp had been a Sergeant, and the leader of the Patrol that night in the jungle had also been a Sergeant.

The officer standing by the desk turned as another armed Sentry and two orderlies came down the hall. The officer nodded the arriving men's attention to the stretcher on the gurney by the wall, then strolled over and joined them beside it. The officer held their attention for several minutes by going through the information from the papers he had been given, gesturing and pointing as he talked.

When the officer had finally finished he turned and headed across the small rotunda. The two orderlies took charge of the stretcher and followed the newly arrived Sentry, maneuvering around the desk and into the hall on the far side.

Jamie stayed above the stretcher as the two orderlies followed the sentry along the corridor and turned into a short hallway. The orderlies stayed close to the officer and the sentry as they pushed through the batwing doors at the end.

Inside, the large room was divided into half a dozen cubicles, much like an emergency room, only the cubicles were actual rooms, each with the appearance of an examination room. Each room had its own stainless steel work table, much like what Jamie imagined to be a morgue.

Jamie stayed above it all as the two orderlies transferred the stretcher, with the black vinyl bag containing his body, from the gurney to the table and pushed the gurney aside. The officer moved to the table, but paid no attention to the body as he began to go over the papers again; the papers that the officer who had accompanied the body had given him.

With the man engrossed in his reading, the sentry, the one who had been stationed in the hall, turned at a soft knuckle rap on the door. He opened it and admitted two men who were wearing white coats and what appeared to be white paper shower caps.

As the officer briefed the two men they nodded

knowingly, each of them meticulously pulling on a pair of white rubber gloves. Then when the officer had left and took the two orderlies with him, the two newly arrived men stood side by side at the table and began to slowly scan the sheaf of papers themselves.

When they had finished with the papers, they talked back and forth for a minute as each of them carefully fitted a surgeon's mask over their nose and mouth, then made sure their rubber gloves were secure.

The one on the far side of the table leaned forward and carefully worked his arms under the body bag and lifted it while the other one slid the stretcher free and placed it back on the gurney by the wall.

Jamie moved closer, hovering just above them as the two men carefully straightened the body bag, positioned it squarely on the table and reached for the zipper.

Chapter Twenty-Eight

Jamie moved closer as he watched the man slide the zipper all the way down to the foot of the bag. He wanted to make sure the men were careful with the body as they removed it from the vinyl bag. Wanted to make sure they didn't harm it any more than it already was, and, too, he wanted to see what the body looked like after all this time. He knew it would be sent home in a sealed casket, but he just wanted to see if it was still recognizable. He had no doubt that it was his body, but he wanted to see it, wanted to make sure before they went any farther.

As he waited, watching closely, the man turned and picked up a small straight knife, with a thin blade, from the stainless steel topped table behind him. He leaned over the bag at one end and deftly cut it across from the zipper to the outer side, and then the other. He folded each side back, letting it drape over the edge of the table.

Jamie was relieved that they apparently weren't going to try to move the body, and were just going to unwrap it where it lay.

The large dried leaves were still intact, tightly enmeshed except for the two small openings that had been made on arrival here. He could see the faded camouflage material of the fatigues through the opening at the chest, and the dried, cracked leather of the shoe protruding through the opening at the left foot.

He watched the two men each drag a large, round open container from the corner and position them next to the table beside them. They both gave their rubber gloves a tug and leaned over to begin examining the leaves more closely, apparently speculating on the best way to start removing them without damaging either the clothing or the body.

Jamie continued to hover close even though he had begun to realize that he didn't remember that he really couldn't be sure of what his body was supposed to look like anymore.

He had never been one to spend much time in front of a mirror, except to shave and wash his face. And he had never spent any time scrutinizing what few pictures of him that had been taken, especially the one in the high school graduating class yearbook. He couldn't really remember the picture anymore, just that he hadn't been too happy with it.

Then he began to think about all the time that had passed since that day in the jungle when he suddenly realized he had been released and had risen from his body. And without the need for a body anymore, he had harbored no thoughts of trying to remember much about it except that he wanted it buried with his family. He wanted Momma and Poppa, and certainly Rosemary and Jodie to understand why he hadn't returned home when the war was over.

Jamie hovered above the body, between the two men but high enough to be out of their way, when he began to realize he could make out what they were saying as they peeled away a leaf. It was one of the large leaves that had been partially turned back before to examine his fatigues.

The one man held the large leaf up to the light and examined it carefully for several minutes, then draped it over the rim of the large round container behind him and turned back to the body.

He pointed to the conspicuous slit in the front of the fatigue blouse without touching it. "Look at this, Frank. The guy was apparently bayoneted. This wound is about the width of a bayonet blade, and the dark stain around it is probably blood. We'll check it to be sure. Might even be able to type it."

Jamie suddenly felt comfortable with the two men. They were the first ones to make any attempt, or even mention identifying the body.

The two men peeled back another leaf slowly, proceeding with extreme caution as they worked. On removal of a third leaf, Frank leaned down and scrutinized another slit in the front of the tunic, this one to the left side of the body and slightly lower than the first one.

"Here's another one, Abner." Frank studied the slit a moment before he looked up. "But there's no stain around this one."

Jamie moved down, closer but still above the body for a better view, looking down between the two men. He hadn't thought to examine the body while it lay there in the jungle, but he did remember that all four of the other guards had eagerly taken a turn to charge across and shove their bayonet into his body before he could manage to scare them off.

The two men were overly solemn now as they carefully removed several more the large leaves, exposing the faded fatigue jacket from side to side, and from the collar down to its bottom hem.

They both stopped and stood somberly, frowning quizzically down at the body when they had discovered that there were four more bayonet holes in the jacket, in addition to the blood stained one.

"My God." Abner spoke softly, almost reverently, shaking his head as he looked down at the blouse for a moment before he turned away. "What could have possibly brought that on? Bayoneted four times after he was already dead."

When he finally turned back to the table, he noticed that Frank had stepped over to the desk, picked up the phone and dialed a number, and stood there waiting for an answer.

Jamie took the opportunity to examine his body more closely while the one called Frank made his phone call.

"Hello, this is Frank. Tell Captain Manwaring that we've started unwrapping the body and have run into something very unusual, something that he needs to know about, needs to see." He listened for a moment then nodded as he continued. "Yes. We've run into something down here that I'm sure he'll want to see."

The two men waited by the table, stolidly folding back the edges of the leaves that were still intact around the opening, tucking them out of the way to make sure all five of the slits would be easy to see.

Jamie was as shocked as the two men at the table. He had never really thought to look at the damage the other four guards had done. He was too intent on scaring all of them away.

The Captain cautiously opened the door as though he didn't know what to expect, then reached back to push it shut behind him and warily approached the waiting men.

"Have you identified the body?" His words were hesitant. "Found something we can work with?"

"No, Sir. Not yet." Frank raised a finger to point as he turned to the body. "We're not too optimistic about getting any kind of a fingerprint, and we haven't gotten far enough to consider the dental yet, but we thought you might want to take a look at this."

The officer leaned closer as Frank pointed, scrutinizing the blood stained slit first and then the other four. "It would appear that this GI was bayoneted, notice the one blood stained hole in his jacket, then bayoneted four more times postmortem."

The officer gravely leaned over the body, closely examining the openings in the faded fatigue jacket. After a long moment he straightened up and turned to Frank with a sudden harshness.

"There have been rumors for years that live prisoners of war were used for bayonet practice back in those days, but we've never had any kind of real proof." The officer stepped back, his voice becoming even more stern as he talked. "I want that blouse removed very carefully, careful enough that those entry slits and any related exit slits in the back remain intact, and I want an identity on this soldier, and I want all of this yesterday. That's a direct order, soldier."

Frank blinked at the sudden change in the Captain's bearing as he turned slowly toward Abner.

The Captain didn't wait long enough for the two men's eyes to even meet, his voice still sharp. "Understood."

"Yes, Sir." Frank fumbled a salute as he stepped back from the adamant officer. "We'll get right on it, Sir. And we'll see if we can get any kind of a print from his hands."

The Captain nodded sharply and turned toward the door, then stopped without turning as Frank continued.

"And we'll see what we can get for a dental."

"Very good." The officer nodded quickly as he reached

for the door handle. "And if anybody gives you any 'who said', any kind of flack at all, get their name, rank and serial number and give me a call."

"Yes, Sir." Frank saluted sharply this time and turned back to the table, even though the officer was gone and the door had closed.

Chapter Twenty-Nine

Jamie rose to the ceiling where he could watch both men, Frank on one side and Abner on the other. They both had turned back to the body and began to carefully peel the clinging leaves away along each side, exposing the sleeved arms and the shriveled clenched hands.

When they had the arms freed, Frank slowly rolled the body to its right and held it as Abner slid the blouse from the left shoulder of the withered corpse and gently down the stiffened left arm.

Abner took his time as he carefully folded the bulk of the blouse and sleeve lengthwise, and snugged it close to the back of the body then helped Frank roll the body over onto its left side. Abner now held the gaunt body while Frank carefully slid the blouse from the right shoulder and down the equally stiffened right arm.

Frank reached back and placed the blouse on the stainless steel table behind him and helped Abner lower the body back into place, on its back again. They both stood in awe of the shriveled, leathery skin on the emaciated, mummy like torso, and even the one apparent fatal wound, the one that had bled slightly before the heart stopped beating, was not so discernible anymore.

Abner continued to stand solemnly, watching Frank take the blouse carefully by the shoulders and hold it up for inspection. There were slits in the back of the garment that matched the four unstained slits in the front, as well as the one matching the stained bayonet hole, but showing considerable more staining than the entry wound in the front. The dark stain on the back of the blouse had blossomed farther out into the material, conspicuously showing the small cut made by the apparent protruding point of the blade of the bayonet.

Jamie examined the gaunt torso while Frank carefully folded the fatigue blouse. Frank did it like a laundry folds shirts. He folded it to show the five bayonet holes in the front, then he took a sizeable clear plastic bag and a large, flat paper sack from one of the storage cabinets. He gently slid the faded garment into the bag, then into the paper sack for delivery to the Captain. He lifted it with his hands palm up under the package and headed for the door where Abner stood holding it open.

"Be back in a minute." His voice was soft, but optimistic as he passed Abner. "See if you can find something that will help the Captain get some idea of who this guy is."

Abner just nodded as he closed the door and turned back to the table. With both of the body's arms bare now for the first time, he couldn't help but notice the scarred wrists as he nestled the stiffened, spindly arms alongside the naked upper body. He frowned, studying the scarred wrists as he continued to loosen and remove the leaves along the legs.

Jamie moved in closer, his attention on the toe of the left shoe protruding through the small opening in the cocoon of brown leaves.

The abrasions on the wrists of each arm held Abner's attention as he worked. He would mention it to Frank when he got back. This GI's hands had been bound with something more than just a piece of rope or some kind of vines; something with spikes or sharp uneven edges.

He scowled at the thought of the young soldier strung up on a cross with his hands secured to the horizontal bar with something like barbed wire.

Abner shook the thought from his mind as he uncovered both legs all the way down to the feet. He couldn't help but notice the right leg was straight with the shoe resting on its back with the toe pointing straight up, but the left leg lay at an unnatural angle. And while he was removing the leaves, he had noticed the left foot was splayed outward with the shoe resting on its outer side.

Jamie hovered closer when Abner leaned down to examine the left shoe. The man tried to twist the foot to rest on its back in a more natural position, like the right shoe, but the leg was as stiff as the rest of the body.

Abner didn't want to disturb anything, didn't want to further damage the body in any way before they had even identified it or had a chance to examine it closer. The bayonet holes in the jacket and the scarred wrists certainly attested to undue abuse, but the irregular angle of the left leg and foot indicated that things were not exactly copacetic, that there had been something else drastically wrong; something that could have contributed greatly to this soldier's capture and demise.

When Abner leaned over to better study the left leg and shoe, a faint muffled noise caught his attention, like the soft hoot of an owl. When he leaned further down, closer to the shoe, the sound continued even when he straightened up to look around the room for a moment.

Then when he started to turn back to the leaves, the sound became even more pronounced. Still soft, but persistent and strangely enough, still emanating from the direction of the left shoe

He leaned down to the shoe again and the sound softened a bit, but continued. Abner turned his head slowly back and forth to make sure the shoe was really where it was coming from, then noticed the front of the heel on the shoe had a slight gap between it and the sole. While the heel itself was not new, it was slightly askew, as though it had been taken off and replaced by an apprentice, replaced by someone other than a cobbler.

Abner moved quickly back from the table as the cold thought crossed his mind. *BOOBY TRAP.*

There had been instances of the bodies of missing service personnel being returned that had been booby trapped in some way. He was aware of several reports that abandoned guns and other likely battlefield souvenirs had been booby trapped, and later, there had been instances where some sort of explosive device had been implanted somewhere on or in a returned body, set to detonate on contact.

Abner was still standing there aghast, afraid to even move, when Frank pushed the door open and stepped in.

Frank stopped at the sight of Abner's consternation. "What's the matter? What did you find?"

He started moving slowly forward, the details of his converation with Captain Manwaring brashly superseded by the shock on Abner's face.

Frank stopped when Abner raised a hand to him, palm out, and nodded gravely toward the left foot of the body. "There has been something planted under the heel of the left shoe."

A frown creased Frank's brow. "What kind of something?"

"I don't know." Abner shook his head warily. "But the heel of the left shoe has been removed and replaced rather amateurishly, and I can see a short strip of metal that has been inserted under the heel from the front of it. From the instep of the shoe."

"What does it look like?"

"I didn't try to look too close. There have been people killed with stuff like this. We need Captain Manwaring to have someone check it out before we go any further."

Frank hesitated for the moment it took to fathom what Abner had just said, then he nodded and turned slowly to pick up the phone.

Chapter Thirty

Frank and Abner had stepped out into the hall after Frank's phone call to Captain Manwaring, and were waiting uneasily there by the door when the two Sergeants, with their packs of parapheranalia, hurried down the hall.

Jamie was sorry for all the confusion, but glad they were going to finally find the dog tag he had hidden in his shoe that first night he had been in the bamboo cage.

The memory of GA's whispered advice that night brought back the image of the salt mine where GA and Rebel had ended up. There had been nothing he could do to let somebody know where they were, and their families would probably never know what happened to them.

The thought saddened him while he watched the two Sergeants don their protective gear, preparing for the worst just to recover his dog tag. He had never heard anything about booby trapped bodies, but from the only personal contact he had with the enemy, if the prison camp guards were characteristic of the enemy forces, he didn't blame these people for their caution. He was sorry to cause so much confusion, but glad now that he had left something that they could identify his body with.

Jamie stayed where he was while the two Sergeants moved some long-handled round flat gadgets over the body. He moved higher and over by the back wall when they started using other instruments, some with lighted dials or little blinking red and green lights on them.

They moved their instruments along both sides and over his body again, then began to concentrate on the left shoe.

He was certain there would be no trouble, but the two men's precautions were infectious, and he didn't need any more trouble.

Grandpa Jordan had never gone into anything like this in his stories, nothing about departed souls being harmed by earthly calamities, but Jamie was almost certain that earthly mishaps could no longer affect him. However, he had a long way to go yet to get his body home and didn't intend to take any unnecessary chances.

While he watched from where he was above them, both of the men finally put down their instruments and the one Sergeant took a slim, pointed instrument, resembling a small ordinary screwdriver, from his pack on the table behind him.

Jamie moved closer now that the two men had apparently satisfied themselves that there was nothing to fear, no explosives involved, and had begun to pry at the heel of the left shoe with the flat-tipped instrument. Even though they had apparently satisfied themselves that it was safe, they had hesitated long enough to readjust their tedious aprons, visored helmets and heavy gloves before they leaned down to start.

When they finally had the heel loose enough on the

front side to see what it was, the one Sergeant took a small pair of needle-nose pliers from his pack on the table behind him and reached in carefully to retrieve the dog tag. As it cleared its hiding place the other Sergeant reached out with his gloved hand and took the small piece of metal from the pliers.

As soon as the Sergeant had the dog tag in his hand, he started trying to make out the raised writing. Even while he reached down blindly and took a piece of soft yellow cloth from his pack on the floor and began to wipe at the corroded metal.

Frank leaned forward curiously as he spoke to the Sergeant, then politely took the dog tag, yellow cloth and all, from the Sergeant and turned toward Abner with it. They smiled at each other, showing their relief, then Abner took it and began to wipe away as much of the corrosion as he could while Frank waited.

The two Sergeants both began taking off their protective clothing and putting their equipment back together. Frank made a point of thanking them while they worked, then escorted them to the door, still expressing his gratitude for their help.

Frank had just turned from the door when Abner's eyebrows shot up as he finally stopped rubbing and raised the dog tag to eye level.

"Well, now. It looks like our boy here just might be one Jamison L. McFarron, if this is indeed his dog tag. We now have not only a name, but an ID number and blood type to check out."

Frank reached out anxiously and took the small piece of drab metal, quickly checked the back then turned it around to read the information. He looked at the body, then back at the dog tag as if he were trying to connect the two even though he realized that he had no way of really being sure.

Frank really had no reason to doubt that the tag belonged to this body, so he went over it again, scrutinizing the information. He wanted to be sure before he called Captain Manwaring.

Abner carefully pushed the shoe heel back into place while Frank stepped over to the phone, picked it up and dialed, then stood anxiously waiting for an answer. When the busy signal continued he put the phone down, picked up Abner's piece of yellow cloth to cover the dog tag then turned to the door and left.

Jamie rose higher to where he could follow Frank and still keep an eye on Abner as he took a thin white blanket from a shelf in one of the gray storage cabinets and covered the partially naked body, all except the shoes.

Frank strode determinedly down the corridor and turned into the Captains office, on past the sergeant at the reception desk and hesitated momentarily at the private door. He gave the closed door two quick knuckle raps, then pushed it open and stepped inside.

The Captain lowered the phone at the intrusion, a questioning frown on his face as Frank stopped in front of the desk, beaming as he held the dog tag out like some kind of prize.

"It was a dog tag under the heel of his left shoe, and we can see no reason to doubt that it's his."

"But you're not sure." The Captain turned and gave a quick 'I'll call you back," and cradled the phone.

"Well, no." Frank slowly lowered the dog tag at the Captain's lack of enthusiasm. "No Sir. We haven't unwrapped the body completely yet."

The Captain reached out and took the dog tag, examined it closely for a moment, then looked up. "It's probably his. There have been instances where GI's concealed a dog tag on their person for some reason, but we will need a fingerprint, a dental or something that will connect the information on this tag to this body."

"Yes, sir." Frank nodded. "I can understand that."

The Captain raised the dog tag and shook it slightly toward Frank. "In the meantime I'll have this information," he squinted as he brought the tag down to eye level and moved it closer, "run through the system and see what we can find on this guy."

He studied the tag closely again for a moment. "See what we can come up with on one Jamison L. McFarron."

"Yes, sir." Frank gave a quick two fingered salute as he turned sharply and headed for the door.

Chapter Thirty-One

Jamie watched Frank hurry away down the corridor until he reached the room where Abner waited with the body, then turned back to watch the Captain at his desk. The man studied the dog tag carefully for a moment before he pulled a long yellow tablet over in front of him and began writing down the information.

The large paper sack holding Jamie's fatigue blouse was still there on the front corner of the polished desk.

When the Captain finished writing he slowly read what he had written, then nodded and turned around to an instrument on the credenza behind him. He leaned the yellow tablet against a small stand beside the flat keyboard.

The thing looked to Jamie like a typewriter without a roller for the paper or a return lever, and to the left of the keyboard was a small cabinet with a screen in the front. The screen lit up when the Captain touched a switch on the side, then fingered a couple of keys.

While the captain just sat there, looking at nothing in

particular, Jamie moved closer and hovered slightly above and behind the man, where he could see the screen. Just as Jamie got into position to see, the screen flip flopped and zoomed to life, then stopped with a format for a letter outline, and a little black vertical bar blinking at the start of the address position.

Jamie moved closer as the Captain began punching keys with his two index fingers, his head moving back and forth between the screen and the keyboard while he worked.

When the Captain had finished typing he sat back and studied what he had written on the screen. Finally, he reached out to hit several more keys in rapid succession, then touched a lone key and settled back to wait.

After a short moment another piece of equipment to the Captain's right, another small cabinet with just a slot across the front near the top, came to life and a sheet of paper whined out of the slot with what the Captain had typed on the screen neatly printed on it, yet the message was still there on the screen.

Jamie marveled at the efficiency of the equipment as he rose higher, to hover near the ceiling while the Captain took the sheet of paper and read it. When he finished he gave the page a tri-fold, took a long white envelope from a drawer and placed the folded page and the dog tag in it.

He leaned forward to reach across his desk for the paper sack containing the fatigue blouse, then swiveled his chair around and got up. He stuck the sack under his arm and headed for the door.

Jamie stayed with the Captain as he hurried along the corridor, made a right turn and continued until he came to the door at the end. The Captain slowly pushed the door open and entered a spacious office with a Lieutenant manning the receptionist's desk.

The Captain approached the receptionist's desk, spoke

to the man for a moment, then walked over and took a seat in one of the leather chairs positioned across the room near the wall. The Lieutenant picked up his phone and punched one of the buttons on it. He talked for just a moment, hung up and motioned to the Captain.

The Lieutenant took the Captain into the private office, introduced him to the older man behind the desk and left. Jamie wasn't familiar with the small emblems on the man's collar, but he was sure, from the Lieutenant's and the Captain's deference to the man that he was a senior officer, possibly even the Commandant of the military establishment where they were.

When the proper military courtesies had been taken care of, and the Lieutenant returned to his station, the Captain seated himself in the chair in front of the desk. He talked, gesturing with the envelope for a moment before he handed it across the desk. The officer took it and settled back as he extracted the letter and slowly read it, then took the dog tag out and read it, also, turning it back and forth several times, then read it again.

When the man began to nod his understanding, the Captain took the fatigue blouse from the paper sack, still in its clear plastic wrapper. He stood as he took a silver pen from his shirt pocket to use as a pointer, and moved around to the left side of the officer's chair at the massive desk.

The Captain called attention to the bayonet holes in the garment, particularly the fatal one with the blood stain. Jamie hovered above them as the Captain then pointed out the other four postmortem bayonet holes in the garment and explained what they might possibly indicate. Then, with the man nodding gravely, the Captain explained that he had already forwarded the information from the dog tag he had just read, the one that was found in the shoe of the soldier's body that had recently been recovered.

The older officer questioned the Captain extensively on the details of the recovery, asked to be kept informed, then nodded to the garment as he pushed it back into the large paper bag. He dropped the dog tag back into the long white envelope and handed it across the desk to the Captain.

Jamie could make out their conversation well enough to understand that the older officer was highly incensed over the situation, and was going to take the garment to someone higher up. Someone with the proper authority to demand an explanation through diplomatic channels of the postmortem bayonet holes in the fatigue blouse.

Jamie had no animosity toward anyone after all this time, and wasn't particularly interested in delaying the return of his body. Rosemary and his family had waited long enough.

The Captain put the envelope with the dog tag in his brief case and closed it, stepped away from the desk as he gave the officer a quick salute and headed across the room to the door.

Jamie noticed that higher officers made an attempt to salute each other as he watched the Captain head back to his own office, and at the same time watched the older officer pick up a good sized leather case from the floor beside his desk. The man folded the top of the paper sack over the end of the plastic cover, placed the tri-fold letter on top of it and put them both into the large leather case.

Jamie stayed where he was while the officer made a short phone call then hung up and reached for his cap resting on the small shelf of the coat stand. The scrambled eggs on the visor of his cap impressed Jamie. He had never had any personal contact with the upper echelon of the military, and it was too late for that now. All he wanted to do was see that his body reached home, was delivered to Momma and Poppa, then he would try to figure out what he had to do after that.

The officer clicked the leather case closed, raised his cap to his head and pulled it on determinedly, then picked up the leather case and headed for the door.

Jamie floated along above the officer as he went down the hall and into the elevator. He stayed above the man as he crossed the lobby and went out the side door to an olive drab sedan waiting with the motor idling.

The driver stepped out and opened the rear door when he saw the officer, waited for him to get in, then closed the door and got back in behind the steering wheel. He quickly shifted the car into drive, pulled away from the building and headed for the gate.

Jamie wasn't curious about the small flag on the front bumper of the olive drab car as he stayed above it, or even who the officer was. He was just interested in where the man was going with the fatigue blouse. He was aware that bodies were shipped home in a sealed casket, but he wanted to be sure his was going to be fully dressed when it got there.

Chapter Thirty-Two

Jamie drifted along, staying above the car as it sped across town and turned into the gated entry to a large domed building. The sentry hurried out of his guardhouse as the approaching car slowed, then at the sight of the small flag on the front bumper, stepped back and saluted. The driver moved slowly until they were past the man, then sped up and pulled into one of the reserved parking spaces near the side entrance and stopped. He got out quickly and opened the rear door.

The officer laboriously pulled himself out of the car with the large leather case in hand, nodded his thanks to the driver as he crossed in front of him and entered the building.

Jamie stayed with the officer as he entered the elevator, rode to the third floor and went into an office with what looked like some kind of an official seal on the opaque glass in the door.

When the woman at the reception desk saw the officer she picked up the phone hurriedly and pressed a button, spoke briefly and had hung up by the time the officer reached her desk.

She got up and turned with a smile, waving him to the closed door behind her, and Jamie heard her say, "Go right in, Sir, he's expecting you."

Jamie drifted on ahead, into the large office and hovered above the shiny wooden desk. A distinguished looking gray-haired gentleman sat in a high backed leather chair behind it, his eyes anxiously on the door.

His dark suit, light gray double-breasted vest and wide diagonally striped tie could very well be a diplomatic uniform. The man pushed himself slowly up from the massive leather chair as the door opened and the officer came in with his leather case.

After the greetings and salutations were finally finished the man waved the officer to an armed, leather upholstered chair in front of his desk and lowered himself back into his own chair. He ran his hand lightly over his hair, adjusted his shirt collar, checked his tie, perfunctorily preening, then shot his cuffs and snugged his chair closer to the desk.

Jamie was astonished with the man's arrogant demeanor and the size of his desk that didn't appear to have ever had anything on it other than the shiny gold pen stand and the man's elbows.

The officer leaned forward on the edge of his chair and brought the man up to date on the gist of the situation, and other information he had been given about the recovery of the body, and the dog tag that had been concealed under the heel of the shoe.

Then, when the officer got to the matter of the four postmortem bayonet holes in the fatigue blouse, and what they possibly suggested, the man stifled a yawn as he meticulously placed his elbows on his desk and steepled his fingers in front of his face.

As the officer lifted the faded garment in its plastic cover from his leather case and placed it on the front edge of the polished desk, the man hurriedly pushed his chair back, scowling his revulsion. His scathing eyes raked the officer, then the package as though it were something obscene, as if the audacious officer had just defiled his pristine domain.

The officer scooted the plastic case across the desk, ignoring the man's abhorrence as he explained that they needed him to run it by their Ambassador. The officer further explained that this was the first real evidence our military had managed to get their hands on. Evidence that would verify rumors of the abuse of American prisoners, evidence that during the big war live prisoners of war had been used for bayonet practice.

The man's haughtiness slowly dissolved as he began to realize the seriousness of the matter, and the rank and position of the officer so adamantly pursuing it. He began to nod scornfully as he listened, supposedly agreeing with everything the officer said.

Jamie could sense the man's rejection of the very idea, and what was going through his head. That particular war had been over for a lot of years, and we were now on friendly terms with those people. He could not see jeopardizing that relationship over such a minor incident.

The man continued to nod as if he were in agreement, but Jamie sensed that his mind had already begun to function. Had already begun to formulate a way to avoid a confrontation with the former enemy's Ambassador, yet appease this sanctimonious soldier boy who was merely trying to justify his glorified position in the military hierarchy.

Jamie was appalled at the man's callousness, at such self-serving rationalization and smugness as the man finally gave a relaxed sigh, apparently satisfied with his decision. After all, wasn't that what Ambassadors were trained for. To stifle dissension before it got ugly.

When the officer had finished he picked up his leather case and thanked the man for his time and understanding, then turned to the door. The man walked along with the officer to the door, politely assuring him that he would certainly pursue the matter and keep him informed.

Jamie stayed above the man as he closed the door behind the officer and returned to his desk. The man lowered himself onto the front of the large leather chair and leaned down and took a pair of rubber gloves from a box in the bottom desk drawer.

He took his time putting the gloves on, carefully pulling them over his manicured fingernails, then pulled the large waste basket from under the credenza behind his desk. He leaned down with both hands and lifted a large amount of shredded paper from the container and placed it on his desk.

He glanced at the fatigue jacket where the officer had left it, then started to reach for it as his eyes shot apprehensively to the door across the room. He pushed his chair back and got up, went to the door, quietly threw the deadbolt and returned to his desk.

The man settled himself on the front edge of his chair again, then reached across and picked up the fatigue jacket as though it were contaminated. He scowled, holding it at arm's length while he removed it from the plastic cover and folded it over, hesitated for a moment and folded it over again and stuffed it down into the large waste container.

Jamie watched as he took the rubber gloves off and dropped them in on top of the garment, then took the mound of shredded paper from the desk and returned it to the container. He fluffed it up as if to make sure the garment was completely covered, then shoved the waste container back into its usual place under the credenza.

Jamie stayed where he was as the man went into his private bath room to wash his hands, check his appearance in the mirror, then step back into his office rubbing a dab of lotion into his hands.

The man made sure everything was in its proper position as he glanced around, particularly the large waste container and the plastic cover that the garment had come in was still on the other corner of his desk. He stepped over and took his top coat from a wooden cabinet and just draped it over his shoulders like a cape as he went to the door and stopped.

After one final check to make sure everything was in place, he unlocked the dead bolt, opened the door, flipped off the lights and stepped out into the hall.

Jamie didn't hear any sound like a door lock engaging, but it didn't matter, he would be able to keep watch on the jacket, and there was a sentry in the hall by the door to the room where his body was.

Chapter Thirty-Three

As the light outside began to fade, the building grew dark but it didn't concern Jamie. He had sensed that Frank and Abner covered his body with a white blanket before they left for the night, and he could see the Guard posted outside the door of the room, pacing slowly back and forth in the brightly lit hall.

The building where he was now was quiet for a while after it had become completely dark, then Jamie began to notice sounds of foot traffic and its accompanying noises in the hallway. The cleaning crews with their carts, buckets and other equipment were spreading out to service their assigned sections of the building.

A short dark-complected man with unkempt curly black hair and baggy clothing came around a corner in the hall, trudging along behind his cleaning cart and stopped outside the door. Jamie watched him yawn openly as he glanced up and down the hall, then reach for the knob and push the door open. He reached into the room to turn on the lights, checked the hall again and pushed his cart inside and closed the door. He pulled a ring of keys from his pocket by the long chain attached to his belt, selected a key and locked the door.

The man yawned widely again as he pushed the cart over next to the wall, flipped off the lights and groped his way across to the desk. He pulled the big leather chair back slightly, put a small cleaning cloth over the headrest, then reached down and pulled a bottom desk drawer partially open. He then settled himself into the chair, crossed his feet at the ankles and propped them up on the edge of the drawer.

He blinked as he fumbled with his wrist watch for a moment, then pushed a small button on the side of the case and closed his eyes. He let his head roll back onto the cloth he had covered the soft leather of the chair with, yawned again and relaxed as he drifted off.

The building became quiet again, except for the subdued flush of a toilet somewhere, and the battle of the night traffic in the street below. The wail of a siren overrode the other noises for a moment before it slowly faded away into the distance.

Jamie hovered above the large waste container topped off with the shredded paper the gray haired man had placed on top of the fatigue jacket before he left. He would have thought the man could have found a more secure place than that to hide the garment for the night when a soft muted intermittent buzz began.

Before Jamie could place the buzzing, the man in the leather desk chair roused himself and pushed the little button on his wrist watch, then tiredly lifted his feet from the drawer and kicked it shut. He sat there for a moment before he stood and stretched, then reached over to the wall and turned on the lights and went into the bathroom.

He bent down to the sink and splashed water on his

face, pulled a couple of paper towels from the dispenser
on the wall and came back to the big chair, wiping his
hands and dabbing at his face.

When he finished he leaned down and placed the two
sodden paper towels on top of the shredded paper in the
large container under the credenza, then turned and
went over to his cleaning cart. He withdrew a long
handled push broom, gave the floor a fast going over and
returned the broom to the rack on the cart.

He pushed the cart over to the desk and stopped. He
took the soft cloth from the chair back, gave the surface of
the desk a fast swipe and pitched the cloth onto the cart.
He glanced around for a moment, then stepped over and
picked up the waste basket under the credenza.

Jamie hovered closer as the man took it over to the
rear of the cart, where a large gray canvas trash bag was
suspended from hooks on the inside of the cart handles.
The man upended the waste container into the large bag,
shook it and started to set it down when he noticed a
couple of envelopes stuck in the bottom. He upended it
again, slapped the bottom soundly, quickly checked it
again and replaced it under the credenza.

Before Jamie could fully comprehend what was
happening, the short dark complected man pushed his cart
over to the door, swung it open and pushed the cart
through into the hall, then turned out the lights and pulled
the door closed. He stood there in the hall glancing around
while he pulled a ring of keys from his pocket by the long
chain that was attached to his belt. He took his time
selecting a key, then locked the door, turned to the cart
and ambled off down the hall toward the elevator.

Jamie wasn't concerned with the lick and a promise
cleaning job the man had given the office, he was just
concerned with where exactly the man was going with
the fatigue jacket. He followed along, keeping an eye on

the trash bag while the man arrived at the service elevator, hit the button and stepped back to wait. When the doors finally opened, Jamie stayed above the cart as the man pushed it into the large service elevator and rode it to the basement.

As they left the elevator and crossed the large basement, Jamie noticed the commercial laundry machines the women were operating. There were storage cabinets and other maintenance equipment down there, but he didn't recognize the large structure with its dials and gauges in the far corner of the basement where the man had stopped his cart.

Jamie watched the man twist a lever to the left and swing the heavy door open, then lift the cover on a gaping chute. The man lifted the trash bag from the hooks on the handles on his cart and dumped its contents into the open receptacle. He gave the trash bag a couple of half-hearted shakes over the opening, checked to make sure it was empty, then rehung it on his cart handles and closed the chute.

While the man closed the door and moved the lever back into place, the operation did not register with Jamie. He had never seen a commercial incinerator before, but when the man reached up and hit the large red button, and the needles in the dials began to move, Jamie quickly understood what it was and realized that his fatigue jacket was gone.

He understood now why the gray-haired man had been so particular about hiding the garment in the waste basket like he did. Jamie had sensed that the man was not too happy with the situation, but he would never have thought that a man in such a position of authority would stoop that low.

Jamie watched the dark complected man park his cart against the wall with the others, take a time card from the rack and ring out, then replace the card and head for the elevator at the front of the building.

Jamie couldn't generate any ill feelings toward the little dark haired custodian, but his feelings toward the gray haired man in the fancy clothes was something else altogether.

Chapter Thirty-Four

Jamie stayed there in the basement, hovering beneath the low ceiling, among the jumble of air ducts, steam pipes and electrical wiring, still hurt by the gray haired man's indifference.

He watched the other cleaners come in and empty their trash bags into the same chute where the little black haired custodian had emptied his, where the man had unknowingly disposed of the fatigue jacket hidden under the shredded paper. And the other custodians were all as seemingly unconcerned with the contents of their trash bags as the short, dark complected man had been with his.

By the time the full cleaning force had returned their carts and equipment to the basement, properly stored them and clocked out, dawn had begun to chase away the blackness of the night. Jamie surmised from the foot traffic and the items people were carrying as they came out of the cafeteria and went about their business, that the building was coming alive. The cooks and cafeteria workers had apparently already arrived and had the coffee made and the grills and steam tables ready for business.

And now with the stenographers and office personnel beginning to drift in one or two at a time, some taking time to sit down and eat while others just got a piece of bakery goods or breakfast sandwich to go, Jamie decided not to wait for the gray haired man down here.

Jamie wasn't interested in what the culprit might have for breakfast, and doubted that the man would lower himself to use the cafeteria, anyway, so he drifted up to the office to wait for him there. Everything was just as it was when he and the sleepy little cleaning man had left it late last night.

When the gray-haired man finally arrived, carrying a midsized Styrofoam cup with a lid, Jamie drifted over and hovered above the front of his desk. He watched the man place a folded napkin on the large blotter on his desk and carefully set the apparently hot cup of coffee on it.

The man gently shrugged his topcoat from his shoulders and reached into the closet for a wooden hanger. He took his time hanging the coat, fitting it on the hanger, then turned and went into his private bathroom.

Jamie wasn't surprised at the way the man preened, checking his tie, his hair and profile, turning from side to side, then pushed the door shut with his foot. He stepped back a step and turned from side to side again to check himself in the full length mirror on the back of the door.

When he was apparently satisfied with what he saw, he opened the door and stepped over to his desk. Before he made any effort to sit, he leaned down and checked the large waste basket under the credenza.

Jamie could sense the man's delight at the sight of the empty container. He could almost feel the coarse vibrations of the arrogant man's deceitful contentment.

With an air of smugness the man pulled the big leather chair out from the desk and swung it around sideways and turned with his back to it. He carefully took each trouser leg by the crease with thumb and forefinger at mid-thigh and lifted slightly as he eased himself into the chair and swiveled around to his desk

He prissily took a tissue from the box on his desk and used it to lift the clear plastic cover that the fatigue jacket had been in, when it was brought to him, and placed it on the credenza behind him. Jamie detested the way the man grimaced at the cover, like it was contaminated, then dropped the tissue into the large waste basket, with the same scowl, and turned back to his desk.

Jamie moved closer to the desk as the man reached for the medium sized Styrofoam coffee cup and removed the lid. Jamie waited while the man turned and tossed the plastic lid into the large waste receptacle under the credenza behind him and turned back to lift the steaming coffee cup to his lips. When the cup reached his mouth, even before he had a chance to blow the steaming liquid, a vaporous, whirling vortex suddenly appeared before him in front of his desk.

The man drew back in horror as the vapor slowed and parted to reveal the emaciated body of a young soldier from mid-thigh up. The body was wearing only a pair of camouflage fatigue trousers, bare from the waist up. The eyes were rolled back in its head, the whites only showing in the tormented face and there were five ugly bayonet wounds in the naked torso above the waist.

The wound in the center of the chest had seeped blood until it had trickled all the way down to the waist of the pants, with the other four just gaping wounds attesting to the postmortem brutality and the way the bayonets had been so cruelly withdrawn.

The gray-haired man had recoiled farther, still holding the coffee cup, with his face turning first one way and then the other, as if trying to avoid an intense heat. Then when the gaunt body raised its bony arms and held them out with the palms up, exposing the hideous scarring on the wrists, the man dropped the coffee cup as he fell back in his chair.

The cup hit the blotter at an angle, sloshing hot coffee onto the man's tie, white-on-white shirt and the dove-gray double-breasted vest, then flopped onto its side, allowing the rest of the still steaming coffee to spread out on the leather framed blotter.

As Jamie headed for the door, the apparition faded away, but he didn't look back even though he was aware that the spilled coffee had overrun the blotter's capacity and crossed the narrow leather frame to drip liberally into the stupefied man's lap.

Chapter Thirty-Five

Frank and Abner were just arriving as Jamie drifted in above them in the corridor. He watched them chat with the sentry a few moments before they released him, then continued to chat for another moment before they turned and entered the room.

The two men settled themselves at the desk and talked about what they themselves had discovered about the body so far, discussed the report on where the body had been found, and what they needed to do further to properly identify it.

Jamie didn't know what DNA meant, didn't know about other things they kept referring to, but he did understand their mention of a comparison with his dental records. He had forgotten all about the trips to the dentist, while he was in training, to extract that bothersome wisdom tooth and put a filling in the one next to it.

He stayed above them, appreciative of their concern and respectful handling of the body, especially after his encounter with the gray haired guy in the suit. And he understood why they had to go to so much trouble to properly identify it. Why they needed to match something from his body to the information on the dog tag that GA had suggested he hide in his shoe that night in the bamboo cage, his first night there in the prison camp.

It had never entered his mind that the Army would be so thorough, but then again, he realized how they had to be sure, how they had to be absolutely certain before they started notifying anybody about the recovery of a body, particularly the next of kin.

He understood that they needed to match something from the body to the information on the dog tag. All they really had now was a name, a serial number and a blood type, but no blood. It had all been gone a long time ago, seeped into the ground there in the jungle, except what was on his fatigue jacket.

The gray-haired guy's office came into view but he wasn't there, just cleaning men. One was scouring the desk and chair, where they had been pushed out of the way so the other one could mop the floor.

Jamie had sensed Abner's concern with the appearance of the left leg. The man was definitely concerned with the condition of it, and sure the leg had been damaged in some way before he died.

He watched as both of them finally got up from the desk and started preparing themselves for the work ahead. They continued to talk quietly, discussing what information they had so far. They adjusted their aprons at the neck and tied them adeptly behind their backs, put the surgeon's masks in place over their mouth and nose, then took their time fitting the rubber gloves to their hands.

Jamie could appreciate their concern over the postmortem bayonet holes, and could understand their indignation. He had felt the same way when the other four guards started mutilating his body. He hadn't really thought of it as practice at the time, and after some thought he felt it was more a show of force to keep the other prisoners in line.

But now he would rather they just do what was required, do what they had to do to identify the body and report that it had been found. To let the Army know he wasn't a deserter, then send it on home.

He realized it would be sent home in a sealed casket, but he hoped it wouldn't be without a fatigue jacket, with the body nude from the waist up.

The image of the ambassador, or whatever he was, burying the fatigue jacket in the shredded paper in the waste basket appeared before him again. He had sometimes wondered why Grandpa Jordan was so critical of government officials and politicians, but he understood it better now. He had sensed the man's reluctance to approach something like that after all this time, but that still didn't justify what the man had done.

Jamie didn't know what a tee time was that he had sensed the man was so concerned about while he pondered the imposition that had been foisted off on him, or why it would have something to do with the man's decision to destroy the fatigue jacket.

He understood that it really didn't make any difference with a sealed casket, but with his faith in the Army now restored, he hoped they might possibly put a new dress uniform on his body for its trip home.

Momma and Poppa and Jodie, and of course Rosemary, wouldn't know the difference, but it wouldn't be right to bring his body into the House of God, even if it was for a funeral, without it being properly dressed.

The McFarron family had always dressed respectively to attend Worship Services. Jamie was almost sure that God would not be offended if his body was sent home without a jacket, if it was brought into the church there not properly dressed, but in the position he was in now, so close to finally arriving at those pearly gates, he would rather not chance it.

Jamie moved closer to watch the two men hunched over the body. Frank at the head and Abner by the left hand with some kind of little gadget, like he was trying to imprint or photograph the fingers and the palm, trying to get a picture or impression of the inside of the hand.

The two men were so intent on what they were doing that they didn't hear the Captain come in. Didn't hear him gently push the door closed, then turn and lean his back side against the edge of the desk with his arms folded across his chest.

Jamie could sense the Captain's irritation, but the two men didn't look up until the Captain cleared his throat.

They both stopped what they were doing and turned, then quickly came to attention. Both of them stood rigidly, frowning at the Captain's apparent anger, expecting a reprimand or possibly something even worse, though they were both fairly certain his wrath was not directed at them.

Jamie sensed the Captain's sternness begin to soften at the sight of the two men's subdued manner, at the realization he had allowed his anger to get away from him.

He pushed himself away from the desk as he said, "At ease, men. I didn't mean to startle you, but I've just been informed that this recently recovered GI's fatigue jacket has been inadvertently destroyed."

Both men's bodies wilted, not at the proffered apology and the softened manner, but at the fact that the fatigue jacket, and the possibility of obtaining a blood sample was no longer available to them.

Jamie moved back to the ceiling and drifted into the corner while the Captain talked with the two men. He was not surprised that the gray-haired man in the suit had apparently put together a good enough story.

After a moment the Captain gave each of the men a pat on the shoulder and left, his irritation still evident from the way he closed the door and strode off down the corridor.

Chapter Thirty-Six

The next day, at midmorning, while Frank and Abner were engrossed in removing the rest of the leaves from the body, the Captain came in quietly. He stopped at the desk, a sheet of paper in his hand, a form of some kind, and waited until Frank looked up from across the table before he spoke and stepped over to where they were working.

He handed the form to Frank, then proceeded to explain to both of them that the form was their copy of the information that had been obtained from the specimens they had taken from the body on the table.

Jamie could hear the Captain explaining that the several partial prints, from two different fingers and one of the thumbs, the partials from the left palm and the dental impressions, they managed to get from the body had matched the information on the dog tag they had found in the left shoe.

When the Captain had finished with his explanation, Abner motioned to the wasted left leg and began to explain his theory of its condition.

Jamie was surprised at Abner's rationale of what had probably happened to the leg. The man had apparently examined enough wounds, and other irregularities on returned bodies to be fairly knowledgeable of what occurs in actual combat. He had apparently seen enough of it to be familiar with the degeneracy of man-to-man warfare.

The Captain listened raptly, his facial expressions showing his deep concern as Abner explained that the wound on the back of the left leg had been caused by a poisoned stake, probably a piece of sharpened bamboo. It had been inflicted in some manner not more than a day or two prior to death, as the wound site shows little or no attempt to heal.

Abner slowly turned to the Captain. "Back in that war, in the jungles, open pits, oh, probably no more than a foot to a foot and a half deep were dug in the middle of a narrow jungle trail. Sharpened bamboo stakes with the tips coated with some kind of poison were placed in them, then the pit covered with something flimsy and that hidden by a cover of leaves and other debris from the jungle floor. They had a name for them, which escapes me at the moment, but they were very effective.

When Abner hesitated, and the Captain continued to frown and blink his concern, Frank began to explain that prisoners of war back then almost never received any kind of medical attention. When a prisoner was wounded, or too ill or weak to do their assigned work, or unable to keep up on a forced march to move the prison camp to elude enemy forces, they were brutally wasted and their body abandoned where it fell.

Frank drew in a deep breath and glanced at the Captain, then at Abner and continued. He dropped his eyes back to the shrunken body on the table as he explained that from what he had learned, and saw first hand of the return of this young soldier so far, was appalling.

He turned to look directly at the Captain now as he continued. "From the deplorable condition of the left leg and the hideously scarred wrists, I certainly have no doubt that this soldier was severely incapacitated by the poison from the hidden bamboo stake, and had become a burden. And with their need to hurry on their march through the jungle, for whatever reason, the young man couldn't keep up and was bayoneted." His voice rose slightly. "Brazenly bayoneted five times and his body left to rot where it fell in the jungle."

Frank raised the index finger on his right hand to emphasize the point as he leaned forward over the table, his watery eyes wide and a slight tremor in his raspy voice. "And with four of the bayonet wounds being made postmortem, and the wrists so brutally scarred, I can only surmise that the most honorable guards readily jumped on the opportunity to improve their egotistical finesse in the art of unopposed bayoneting."

Jamie was as spellbound as Abner and the Captain were as Frank slowly turned with his back to them and withdrew a tissue from the box on the table. He shamelessly wiped at his eyes for a moment before they heard the muted apology. "I'm sorry, sir, but it pisses me off."

The room was reverently quiet as Jamie looked at Frank with the same feelings he had that morning for Rebel when the man reached out with his crudely bound crippled hands and grasped his left arm at the shoulder, despite the guard's threatening bayonet, and lifted him from the jungle floor and helped to steady him on his one good leg.

It had continued to bother Jamie that Rebel and GA

were probably still working in that salt mine, wherever it was, and would until the end, then their body's would probably be dumped down a worked-out shaft in the mine and their families would never know what happened to them.

Jamie was still being driven by the task of getting his body home so his family would know what had happened to him; know that he was not a deserter. And also, so they could give his body a proper burial in the family plot behind the white steepled church up there on the side of the mountain.

The thought of ultimately seeing his two friends again, after his journey to return his body to his family was over hadn't occurred to him because he was still working on providing closure for his family. But he hadn't forgotten the fact that he had failed to be able to do anything to help Rebel and GA provide closure for their families.

Jamie watched Frank slowly turn back to the table to face Abner and the Captain as the Captain leaned down to examine the shrunken, leathery left hand, particularly the lacerations around the wrist.

The Captain glanced across at the other wrist for a moment, then, his voice was soft as he leaned closer to the left wrist again. "What could they have possibly used as a restraint that would be that brutal?

Frank was looking down at the hand on his side of the table as he responded. "Barbed wire, sir. And in some instances it was so rusted that the continued use caused such serious infections that, left untended, there was no alternative but to amputate."

The Captain frowned, blinking rapidly as he straightened up and turned to Frank. "Amputate?"

"Yes, sir. When gangrene was in such an advanced stage the prisoner was finally released and arrived back here. When it needed to be done in the prison camp the proper word would be 'chopped'."

Jamie looked down at his body, thankful that it hadn't been mutilated any more than it had, thankful that it was still all there.

Chapter Thirty-Seven

The two men went back to removing the large brown leaves from the rest of the body, still discussing the state of its condition with the Captain. They all three turned when the door opened and a soldier in camouflage fatigues stepped in and handed the Captain a cardboard carton, then turned and left just as quickly as he had come.

Jamie couldn't help but watch the soldier move off down the hall. He hadn't seen a set of fatigues that had been starched and ironed since he had left the training camp. His, and the other new recruits fatigues, weren't even folded when they came back from the laundry.

It sure put him and the other recruits in their place to see their company commander, a Sergeant, so sharp in his freshly starched and pressed fatigues every day, even when they went on bivouac. The lot of them then, except the Sergeant, looked like they had slept in their fatigues, because most of them really did. He had heard comments and remarks on the Sergeant's pajamas, but he had never seen them.

The Captain put the carton on the desk and slowly turned to Frank and Abner, hesitantly getting his thoughts together to explain the box that had just been delivered. He was sure that they were both aware of how a new uniform was packaged, but this one would take a bit of explaining.

Jamie recognized the flat carton, and was pleased, and could understand the Captain's concern after Frank's outburst. Jamie did appreciate everyone's efforts on his behalf, but he didn't want anyone of them to feel they may have possibly been responsible in any way for what had gone wrong with the fatigue jacket.

He watched the Captain look down as he put his finger on the corner of the uniform box. "I could tell you that the powers that be have decided that the least we could do is send Private McFarron home in a new uniform, even though the casket will be sealed." He hesitated a moment before he looked up and continued. "But I won't, because I and the General are as indignant as you will be when I tell you that the fatigue jacket with the bayonet holes was diplomatically cashiered. Not mishandled, not misplaced or lost, but just not considered important enough to chance even a slight tremor in our country's diplomatic relations, after all these years."

Frank's eyes beaded as he began to shake his head in disgust. "Our glorious non-combatant civilian leaders. May the devil claim their hindmost." Then in a softer voice. "Cashier their sorry asses."

Abner drew in a breath, also with abhorrence as he turned to the Captain. "You mean it's gone. That it was intentionally destroyed?"

The Captain began to shake his head slowly. "It was made abundantly clear to me that I am not on the list of

'Need to Know' in this matter. But if I had to venture a guess, I would say that someone with enough authority had sufficient reasons to quash the matter. Felt it was in the best interests of everyone concerned that we not pursue it."

Frank had turned slowly with his back to the table, the tremor in his soft voice again. "Everyone but the young man who was conscripted and abandoned. One of ours who was thrown to the wolves for the proverbial thirty pieces of silver and a pass to the Geisha House."

Jamie rose to the ceiling and moved to the far corner of the room. He hadn't meant to cause trouble, but it did make him feel better to know that there were others who would condemn the guy in the suit if they could only know what he had done.

The air in the room became heavy as the Captain nodded his agreement in silence, then picked up the uniform carton and opened it to examine its contents. While he worked quietly, Frank turned to face the table, and motioned toward the shrunken body.

"Are we going to be expected to put that on the body?"

The Captain quickly shook his head as he refolded the new khaki shirt and carefully placed it on the folded trousers still in the carton. "No." He continued to shake his head as he put the lid back on the carton. "We not only don't have the necessary facilities or the expertise here for preparing a body, we don't have any caskets, either."

Jamie stayed where he was, aware of the instructions that had been given the Captain concerning his body, which were about to be passed on to Frank and Abner. He had developed a trust in Frank and Abner, a lot of respect, but he felt that he was becoming a burden on the two men.

They just nodded while the Captain explained that they were to wrap the body in a shroud that was on its way, then put it in a new body bag, also on its way, and secure it back in the stretcher for transporting to the proper facility in the States.

Frank turned to glance at the wire mesh stretcher standing in the corner as Abner lifted the dangling side of the body bag that they had cut open, studied it a moment and let it fall back with a shrug.

The Captain had moved the uniform carton to the desk as the door opened again and the same soldier handed him two more cartons, which he turned and placed on the table next to the body.

Frank reached over and picked up the one with the large blanket in it and Abner opened the one containing the new body bag.

The Captain waited by the desk, his arms folded across his chest, while Frank picked up the remnants of the fatigue pants they had cut from the body and reverently folded them, then pushed them into the large container on top of the brown leaves.

While Frank shook the blanket out the Captain suddenly turned and left and Jamie moved closer to the table again.

He watched the two men gently roll the body back and forth as they wrapped it in the large white blanket, then folded the corners around the head and feet and secured them with some small metal clips.

The Captain came back into the room while they were carefully putting the wrapped body into the shiny black bag, and waited for them to finish before he handed them a large brown envelope. He explained the situation as they placed the closed body bag in the wire mesh stretcher, positioned it and secured the web straps, then pulled the gurney over from the wall and transferred the stretcher to it.

Abner slid the uniform carton and the large brown envelope down into the side of the stretcher next to the black bag then stepped back next to Frank as an armed guard and two soldiers arrived.

They talked to the Captain for a moment, then nodded to Frank and Abner, took charge of the gurney and headed for the door. As the gurney passed the Captain, he gave a proper salute, but Frank and Abner gave the body a quick two finger salute, then touched the stretcher as it passed and mumbled an apology and a vivid condemnation of the sorry ass who had sold him down the river.

Jamie silently thanked all three of the men as he swung into position over the stretcher. The two soldiers maneuvered it along the corridor, keeping pace with the armed guard walking ahead, oblivious to the small wisp of almost invisible vapor floating above them.

Chapter Thirty-Eight

Jamie stayed above the gurney as the armed guard, walking slightly ahead, reached over and hit a wall button to open the double doors, then stepped aside as the two soldiers brought the gurney through. The guard fell in alongside the gurney as they went down the ramp, onto the tarmac and headed to where the large plane had turned and stopped, waiting with its aft ramp lowered for loading.

The two soldiers and the guard, with the help of two other soldiers in fatigue pants and green T-shirts who were working with baggage in the area, moved the gurney up the ramp and into the plane. Jamie stayed just above the stretcher. He didn't like the idea of his body leaving the building, and certainly not being taken on a journey somewhere in nothing more than a blanket, even though it had been enclosed in the body bag.

When the Captain mentioned that they didn't have the necessary facilities for dressing or preparing a body, Jamie thought he just meant the section where Frank and

Abner were, and that they were only going to take the body to another part of the same building.

Jamie had grown up in a strict family environment where you never walked around the house in your night clothes or underwear or any other state of undress. You were expected to be fully dressed and ready to meet the day when you arrived at the breakfast table. The only time you were allowed to remain in your night clothes during the day was if you were ill, or injured, and was going to return to bed, or at least not going to leave the house at all that day. And even then you had to be wearing your house slippers and a robe over your pajamas.

He couldn't even begin to guess how many times he had heard Grandpa Jordan, and even Momma and Poppa say that naked body parts had no business past the bathroom or bedroom, and especially that bare feet had no place in the dining room.

Jamie watched them fasten the webbing straps across the body bag, then secure the stretcher to the brackets along the wall. The guard thanked the four soldiers as they left, quickly checked their work, then took a seat across from the stretcher.

He slid his overnight bag under his seat and opened the briefcase on his lap to examine the contents of the large brown envelope. He pulled the contents out slowly onto the divider partition in the briefcase, then picked up the shiny bracelet that was enclosed in a small clear plastic bag, smiling as he read the instructions on the tag. To be returned to next of kin. Then he squinted and leaned closer to read the inscription again, Rosemary and Jamie. It touched him to think of it being returned to the wife, fiancee or girl friend who had evidently given it to the soldier when he shipped out.

The smile slowly dissolved into a somberness as the

guard thought of the times, on these trips, that he had encountered grieving widows and children, distraught fiancées, and even sorrowful girlfriends. Years ago, when he first started as a guard he thought of death as the end of a love affair, but he had quickly learned how wrong he was on that. He had begun to realize that to a lot of the survivors the deaths were merely an interlude until they could meet again. So many of the wives never remarried, drawing themselves into a celibacy, never entering into a social life again.

He was even aware of a couple of instances where the girl friend had gone on to live out her life, alone, happy with the memory of her lost love until they could be together again. He stared off into space for a moment, not sure he understood something like that, but he couldn't believe it either.

Jamie watched the guard return the contents to the big envelope, twist the string around the two cardboard tabs, then close the briefcase and set it beside his seat.

The pilot had taxied to the head end of the runway and turned, revving the engines, ready for take off when the tower gave him the word.

The guard leaned down, moving his attention from window to window to see where they were, but Jamie had risen to where he could see the entire airfield and the approaching plane that the pilot was obviously waiting for.

When the arriving plane finally touched down and crossed the take off lane, the pilot revved the engines again and started moving down the runway. He gathered speed quickly as he ran, then lifted off and went into a wide turn to head out over the vast ocean.

Jamie remembered hearing the word 'states' mentioned and was sure that was where they were headed, and was happy about that, but things weren't really going to suit him. If Momma and Poppa, and maybe even Rosemary, were going to be there to meet the plane, Jamie hoped the Army would at least stall them long enough to allow the people there to dress the body and put it in a casket, even though he was sure the casket would be sealed. Nakedness was still embarrassing to him.

The big plane had settled into a monotonous drone with the ocean so far below, and the few people on board either settled down to sleep, or had their little light on above the seat, and were reading or working on some kind of instrument with a small lighted screen and a keyboard.

Jamie moved over to the stretcher and settled down. The uniform box was still there, but the big brown envelope was gone. He hadn't seen the guard take it from the stretcher, but guessed it was okay for him to have it. It was probably just as safe in the guard's briefcase as it was in the open stretcher, but it bothered him that he had failed to notice the guard removing it from the stretcher.

As dawn began to lighten the sky ahead of them, Jamie could see that they had left the ocean and were now over land, the little lights far below twinkling as the country began preparing for another day.

It was good to have his body back where it belonged, headed for home even if it hadn't been dressed yet. He thought of how many times he had heard Grandpa Jordan say that he had come into this world naked and broke and he was going out the same way.

A subdued glow, like the back lighting in a funeral parlor, enveloped Jamie at the thought of his body finally making it back home, then, with his job finished, the possibility of seeing his Grandpa again.

Chapter Thirty-Nine

Jamie couldn't make any sense of where they were at any given time as the plane continued across the vast continent. He could see the rivers and the dual lanes of interstate highways, a desert and a large canyon, several sprawling metropolitan areas with their swarming traffic and lighted capitol domes. The plane finally began its descent, circling the spacious airfield in the army base below, then chose a runway and touched down, the tires screeching their protest on contact with the tarmac.

The sudden reverse thrust of the turbine engines slowed the plane until the pilot could stop, then turn and taxi across to a large building setting off to the right. It was away from the constant traffic between the runways, passenger terminals and the service hangars.

When the plane reached the building the pilot slowly swung the large plane around to face the way it had come and shut down the engines. The whine of the loading ramp being lowered greeted the quietly approaching ambulance with the large red cross painted on its top and smaller ones on each side.

Two attendants in white got out of the ambulance, opened the rear door and took out a collapsible gurney. They unfolded the undercarriage and headed up the planes ramp where they were met by the armed guard.

They both nodded as the guard briefed them while he removed the large brown envelope from his briefcase, discussed its contents with them, then returned it to his briefcase. The three of them continued to talk for a few moments, then the guard turned and led them into the plane where the stretcher, with its black body bag, waited.

The guard stepped back out of the way while the two men released the stretcher from the wall brackets and lifted it to their gurney. The guard   followed along as they went down the ramp to the rear of the ambulance.

They swung the rear door open and lifted the stretcher into the ambulance, properly secured it, then collapsed the running gear on the gurney and returned it to its place along the wall. When the guard had climbed in beside the stretcher, let down the folding seat and settled himself on it, they closed the rear door and returned to their seats in the front of the ambulance.

They pulled slowly away from the plane and headed for a rear exit and crossed into another part of the huge Army Base.

Jamie stayed above the vehicle as it wound its way through the gated compounds and drove around to the back of a somber building, then swirled slowly around and backed up to the dock. Two men in whites came out of the padded swinging double doors, pushing their own gurney while the driver and the other man got out and opened the rear door.

The two men from the ambulance reached in and gave the guard a hand as he got up and duck walked to the back of the ambulance and stepped down. The two other men moved to the edge of the dock and gave them a hand lifting the stretcher to the gurney, then walked alongside as they all turned and entered the building.

Jamie stayed above the gurney, just a small wisp of vapor floating inconspicuously as they moved along the corridor. He was surprised that word must have preceded them somehow when one of the men from the building asked the guard if this was the one that had supposedly been used for bayonet practice.

The guard just nodded as he raised his briefcase and explained that all the information pertaining to the body was in the envelope he had brought along. The two men from the ambulance had apparently not been given too much information on the incident, just what they had managed to get from the scuttlebutt, and from other's questions about what was being done about it.

Jamie appreciated their concern as they stopped in the middle of the corridor, aghast at what the guard had just told them about the missing fatigue jacket that he had read in the information in the envelope. Jamie just wanted them to put the new uniform on the body, put it in a nice casket and send it on home.

All the animosity in the world was not going to change anything, even though he still loathed the prison camp guards for their brutality, as well as the gray haired man who had purposely destroyed his fatigue blouse.

He didn't question these men's resentment while each of them gave their heated opinion on the matter as they began to move solemnly along the corridor again. They were entitled to their opinion, but they were just dogface soldiers like him. Even the Captain who was not on the 'need to know' list and that General who trusted the man in the suit with the fatigue jacket had no recourse in the matter.

Jamie stayed close as they turned into a sterile room with a stainless steel table in the center. It had little gutters all around with drains at the corners and the glass cabinets along each wall contained an array of instruments that had to be surgical.

The two men from the ambulance finally said their goodbyes, shook hands all around and left.

While the guard took the large brown envelope from his briefcase and set the case back on the floor, the two men lifted the body bag from the stretcher and placed it on the stainless steel table.

As the guard surrendered the envelope to them, he explained that his instructions were only to escort the body to where it was now, then inquired as to what was in store for the body from here.

Jamie dropped down to hover just above the two men's heads. He was happy to hear that their only instructions were to dress the body and seal it in a flag draped casket for shipment to the soldier's next of kin.

When the guard asked about any ceremonies that were planned for the body, the two men told him that they weren't aware of any. They said their understanding was that when the family was notified of the recovery of the body, they had insisted that the body just be forwarded to their home.

In reply to the guard's query of where the soldier's home was, the two men just shook their heads and said they didn't know, but wherever it was, the body would go by rail, with an honor guard.

Jamie drifted to the ceiling, out of the way, satisfied with Momma and Poppa's decision.

Chapter Forty

Jamie stayed where he was, high enough to be out of their way as they turned to the table again to finish their work. He was amazed at the condition of the body, even as emaciated as it was, and how good it looked in a new dress uniform, except the face. The two men had made no attempt to reconstruct or even improve the condition of the face.

He realized there wasn't a whole lot they could do with the face, or any of the other parts, really, but the rest of the body was covered by the dress uniform, with a pair of white gloves on the hands.

When they were through with the cutting and fitting, had finished tucking the edges discreetly into place under the body, they gave the uniform one last check. Then, just before they closed the casket, they unfolded a piece of white linen cloth and placed it over the shriveled face, then gently closed the lid. The one man took a small tool of some kind out of a drawer, similar to a small allen wrench, and inserted it into each of the four holes along the front of the casket and twisted it to secure the lid.

Then, while they draped a large American Flag over the casket, and neatly folded it around the ends and corners and clipped it into place, Jamie thought about the cloth they had placed over the face, the only part of the body not otherwise covered. It was probably standard procedure with a sealed casket. He wasn't worried that Momma or Poppa would try to open the casket, but Jodie was something else. His little brother was not mischievous, but he had always been very inquisitive. Jodie was just meticulous, obsessed with a compulsion to see that everything was done right, especially where his family was concerned.

And 'family' to Jodie had finally evolved to include Rosemary. He had recognized her as his adopted sister until her and Jamie began to get so serious, then he began to speak of her as his sister-in-law.

Jamie felt that inner glow again as he thought about his little brother. While Jamie was at home on his training leave, before he shipped out, Jodie had told him not to worry, that he would watch over his sister-in-law while Jamie was gone.

Jodie saw things the way he wanted them to be, and he was happy about Rosemary going to be part of the family. Jodie just didn't see how a piece of paper, a marriage license, could improve how Jamie and Rosemary felt about each other. It would just be to legalize their relationship, something Jodie knew they would need before Momma would even consider letting Rosemary share Jamie's room, before she would even think of allowing them to sleep together in her house.

Jamie's reverie was broken as the two men slowly rolled the casket on its trolley over near the double doors leading to the corridor, checked the flags tautness again, then settled into the chairs at their places at the counter beneath the cabinets on the wall.

The one man went through the contents of the large manila envelope for a moment, then picked up the phone and hit several buttons. He started talking when the call was answered, informing them that the casket was ready, then just settled back in his chair to listen.

He nodded occasionally, asking nothing and volunteering nothing, then acknowledged the information he had been given with a sharp, 'Yes sir'. He reached over and replaced the phone in its cradle, returned the material to the large envelope and turned to the other man beside him.

Jamie moved over and hovered above them when the man leaned closer to the other man and began to share the information he'd been given. "They'll be here for the casket in about an hour. They're going to drive it back to the airport, where it will be taken by chopper to the train station in Millerville, which is about fifty miles north of where the soldier's family still lives."

The other man blinked at the information. "Today? You mean there's not going to be any kind of service here for the poor guy?"

Jamie was happy with what he had just heard. He had hoped there would be no military ceremonies anywhere, that they would just ship the body home, and Momma and Poppa would have it quietly buried in the family plot without a lot of fuss. He was sure that Momma and Poppa, as well as Rosemary and Jodie, would want the pastor of the church to say a few words, would want him to conduct a private ceremony at the cemetery, and that was okay. He just didn't feel that anything more than that would be warranted.

The first man continued while the other one shook his head in dismay at the absence of any kind of military service for the soldier.

"The family's instructions were to send the body home by train, and they even told them which train, and from where that train emanates, and as I understand, the brother made it abundantly clear that he will meet the train and take it from there."

"Where's, there?"

Jamie felt the warm glow again at the thought that Jodie was acting for the family, and could understand the two men's confusion. City people just didn't understand country folks. Didn't understand how anyone could be happy living their lives without all the hustle and bustle of the city.

The first man began to shake his head. "I wasn't given too much detail, but from what little I did get, the railroad was the family's choice, even though there is not even daily rail service any more where they live, and even then it doesn't include passenger service."

"You mean they're going to ship the body home on a freight train?"

The man nodded. "Apparently so. The train only runs on Tuesday and Friday anymore, and the railroad has agreed to put an extra box car on Friday's schedule just for that purpose."

The second man shrugged his disapproval, but Jamie was satisfied with the arrangements.

"Then the railroad people are apparently aware of what the cargo is going to be, but do they know where 'there' is?"

The first man nodded again. "They said the engineer is familiar with the country, and knows the family, and has no doubt that the brother will know where to meet the train."

Jamie could envision the narrow gravel road that came down the mountain from the white steepled church and crossed the lone set of railroad tracks at the big spreading oak tree.

It sounded good to Jamie. The little tail of vapor above the men began to glow intermittently, like a lightning bug, at the mention of Jodie.

Chapter Forty-One

Jamie hovered just below the ceiling of the railroad car, above the casket, becoming more apprehensive with each mile of the rhythmic clacking of the iron wheels on the sectioned track. He had waited so long for them to find his body and send it home, and now that they were on the last leg on the journey, he wasn't too sure that he had done the right thing.

He didn't want to upset his family all over again, and surely not Rosemary, but he didn't want to leave his body out there in the jungle, either, on the other side of the world.

His concentration was broken, as well as that of the Sergeant and the Corporal, the Honor Guards, who had finally settled down for the trip ahead, when the door in the end of the car swung inward. They watched the brakeman, in his dark blue, brass buttoned suit and round visored cap, step through and close the door.

"You guys doing okay?" He looked back and forth from the Sergeant to the Corporal. " You need anything?"

"No, sir." The Sergeant pushed himself up from his chair. "But we're not exactly sure of what we need to do when we get there. The Corporal and I are not trained Honor Guards, we were grabbed from the Recruiting Station at the last minute to escort this soldier home."

The brakeman raised his cap with a smile, finger combed his hair back and replaced the cap all in one motion. "Well, sir." He nodded to the flag draped casket. "It's been many a year since I was in the military, and I never done any honor guard duty, either, but I don't expect there's gonna be any kind of ceremony involved here, anything more than stop the train, turn the coffin over to the family, and be on our way."

"That's about all they told us, too." The sergeant shrugged as he checked with the corporal. "We were told to stay with the casket until the family took charge of it, stay for the funeral if the family prefers, otherwise stay on the train, lay over and come back on the return trip."

The brakeman nodded. "That's what I do. There's a nice little hotel where I stay. We'll get there early Saturday morning, lay over until afternoon, and get back to Millersville late Monday."

Jamie hoped the two guards surrendered the casket to the family without getting off of the train. There was really no need for them to get off, but if they did stay with the casket, for some reason, he was sure that Momma and Poppa would put them up until the train came back on its return schedule Monday.

The sergeant nodded, but still inquisitive. "Do you know where the family is going to meet the train. I didn't get the idea that it would be at a station, or even a town?"

"It won't," the brakeman shook his head. "I'm not all that familiar with this part of the country, but Fred, the engineer, is. He's been on these runs for a lot of years, and knows most of the folks around here. He talked to the family, well, the younger brother who's handling things, and they agreed on where the brother will meet the train to pick up the body."

"And he didn't tell you?"

The brakeman just shook his head. "Fred's been operating trains through these hills for many years, the old steam locomotives and then the diesels when they came along, and he has always operated on a need to know system. He just said that he'll give me a signal when he starts slowing down, and I'm to come back here to tell you guys to start getting ready."

"What's to get ready?" The corporal shrugged. "If we're not going to get off the train, all we gotta do is unload the casket, turn it over to whoever is there, and be on our way."

The sergeant turned sharply to the corporal. "I told you I'll handle it. You just stay out of the way, keep your mouth shut and wait for my instructions. Okay?"

The brakeman stepped farther into the car at the Sergeant's censure, and turned toward the Corporal. "I'm afraid there might be more to this than just delivering an item of freight, Sonny. From what I hear this soldier has been MIA for a lot of years, and there'll probably be family and more'n likely a passel of concerned friends when we get there, and, as a representative of the railroad, I must insist that we all conduct ourselves with the respect this soldier deserves."

The man stopped and drew in a tremulous breath. "There's a native son in that casket who is a returning hero to these people. We will handle this transaction with all the respect and dignity that this soldier has earned, show the same consideration that these people have for him."

The Corporal backed up a step, glanced cautiously at the Sergeant and looked down. "I didn't mean any disrespect, sir. I was just talking."

"That's al'right, young man." The brakeman nodded as he placed his hand on the Corporal's shoulder. "You'll understand these things better after you've been through a baptism of fire, after you've been in a predicament that leaves you no other recourse but to ask the Man up yonder for a little help."

Jamie had floated back into a corner of the box car, not to get away from the attempt to reprimand the Corporal, but because of the short blast of the diesel horn and the decrease he had sensed in power.

The slowing of the train brought the scene back that Jamie had envisioned off and on since they had left the station. The scene of the country ahead, where the gravel road winds its way down from the mountain and crosses the railroad tracks, and the small crowd waiting there in the shade of the big oak tree.

He hadn't been able to recognize anyone in particular, not even Jodie or Poppa, though he was sure they would be there, but he still harbored a bit of self-reproach at the thought that he had let them down, that he had failed in his duties as a soldier.

When the train had finally stopped and the air brakes vented their relief, the brakeman unlatched the sliding door at the side of the box car and slid it open. He told the two soldiers to stay where they were, then turned and went out the door in the end of the box car and down the metal steps from the small platform at the end of the car.

Chapter Forty-Two

The Corporal moved to the side of the open door as the Sergeant moved around the casket, making sure the flag was still in place and the casket had not shifted on the wooden carrying skid.

The Corporal shrugged as he turned from the open door. "I don't see anything out there but a farm wagon with a team of mules. There's nothing else but some men in overalls, a saddled horse and a couple of mules with nothing on them but a bridle.

Jamie hovered lower, out of instinct, so he could see out the open door, but he still didn't see Poppa, and there were no women that he could see, either. He studied the little gray-haired man on the driver's seat of the wagon for a moment before he realized it was his little brother. Jodie's cowlick was still there, the oversized built-up shoe on his left foot, and the same determined look on his face as he flicked the reins to swing the mules into a wide U-turn to bring the wagon into position to back up to the train.

Jodie looked back for a minute to study his position, then began talking softly to the mules and pulling on the reins, backing the wagon up to the open door of the box car.

The Honor Guards, and two railroad men who had hurried into the box car when the train stopped, maneuvered the flag draped casket on its skid across the floor of the box car to the door.

Two of the overalled men waiting in the shade of the large tree had followed the wagon and fallen into place on each side of it as Jodie backed it into place at the open door.

Jodie pushed himself up from the wagon seat and wound the reins around the bracket on the headboard as the two men, one from each side, climbed up into the wagon and positioned themselves to take the end of the skid and move the casket into the wagon bed.

Then, as Jodie turned toward the back, the third man who was now standing by the wagon, the one who had directed Jodie as he backed the team of mules to put the wagon in place at the door of the boxcar, held up his hand. "No, no, Jodie. Stay where you are. We'll take care of this."

Jodie had raised his bad foot to the short lever to set the wagon's brakes, and was in the act of climbing over the wagon seat, but stopped and looked up. "I just need to see that everything's al'right. I don't intend for anything to go wrong for Jamie now."

"We'll handle it, Jodie. You just stay where you are and keep the mules quiet. We'll take care of it back here."

Jodie nodded and steadied himself on the small arm at the end of the seat, then glanced sideways over his shoulder. "Don't worry about the mules. They always go to sleep as soon as they're allowed to stop. They're not going to go anywhere."

A small wisp of vapor moved out of the railroad car, staying high enough to blend with the cloudy sky as the two men in the wagon took hold of the end of the wooden skid. They moved carefully back until the two soldiers and the two railroad employees could lower the other end from the floor of the box car and settle it firmly into the wagon bed.

The overalled man waiting by the wagon moved back and took a length of thin rope from the wagon bed and secured it to the short stake at the rear of the wagon's side board, then slid it across the rear of the casket skid and secured it to the wooden stake on the other side. The other two overalled men began passing short lengths of rope through the outer rail of the casket skid and securing them tightly to the short stakes along each side of the wagon bed.

When Jodie was satisfied that the casket was secure, he released the brake lever, unwound the reins and settled himself into the wagon seat. The two men in the wagon bed moved back, as the wagon moved away from the railroad car, and settled themselves in the end of the wagon bed, their backs to the casket with their legs dangling below.

The other two walked off across the road to the shade of the towering oak tree, where the tall wiry man in tapered denims and a khaki shirt, waited, holding the bridle of a saddled big brown horse. The legs of his denims were stuffed into a pair of brown western boots, and his face was shaded by the brim of a brown western hat that was pulled low over his eyes.

He also held the reins of two unsaddled mules and relinquished them to the men after they had retrieved their shotguns to be ready to go.

The brakeman had climbed back aboard the train and stood with the other two railroad men and the Honor

Guards in the open door of the empty box car. He watched the wagon move away from the train, wanting to be sure everything was in order before he gave Fred the signal that the delivery had been completed satisfactorily and they could be on their way.

"Looks like they're going to do okay without us." The Sergeant commented as they watched the wagon move away from the side of the train and stop in the middle of the narrow gravel road.

The brakeman nodded as he raised his cap, combed his hair back with his fingers and replaced the cap as he watched the care these men were taking with the casket. The two in overalls, who had walked across the road, had retrieved their shotguns from where they had left them leaned against the big tree, then each one took the reins of one of the mules from the man by the horse.

Each of the men lead their mule toward the road, then stopped and pulled himself up astraddle the animal. They waited while the tall thin man in the western hat turned and slipped his left boot into the stirrup of the saddle on the big brown horse, then reached up and nimbly swung himself up into the saddle.

With one short, shrill blast from the engineer, the big diesel engines began to rev up, moving the train forward slowly as the slack from the cars couplings was eliminated with a string of clacking sounds. As the train picked up speed the two soldiers stepped back from the door and the brakeman slid it shut and set the locking lever.

As the train moved away, Jodie waved his thanks then turned around and settled himself into the wagon seat and picked up the reins as he again released the brake lever.

With one final look around, when he was sure everything was to his satisfaction, he glanced over to where the man in the saddle of the big brown horse waited, still in the shade.

Jodie's voice was soft, almost timid as he raised his eyes to the man on the big horse. "Let's take him home, Lester."

The man gave a slight nod as he reached up to tug at his hat brim, then leaned forward and pulled a long barreled squirrel rifle from its scabbard hanging from the front of the saddle.

As he balanced the gun across the horse's withers with his right hand, he held the reins lightly with his left hand, guiding the sprightly animal with his knees. The big horse gave a short lurch, raising momentarily up on its hind feet, then moved from the shade, out into the middle of the gravel road and turned toward the mountain.

The big horse pranced sideways, setting its pace to match that of the slow moving wagon as the two men on the mules fell in at the rear of the procession. In the absence of a saddle the men's legs dangled on each side of their mules, with their shotguns pointed skyward, the stock resting on the thigh of their right leg.

As the mules moved the wagon slowly along, their heads down, their long ears lolling lazily, Jodie reached back and patted the corner of the flag-draped casket. His voice just above a whisper. "Welcome home, Jamie. I can rest easy now."

Jodie raised his arm and drew his shirt sleeve across his eyes as he turned back and settled into the wagon seat for the trip up the mountain to the white steepled church.

He didn't notice the small whisp of vapor that had swirled in behind him and hovered just above the front of the casket.

Chapter Forty-Three

Jodie leaned forward with his elbows on his knees, holding the reins in both hands as he started to talk softly to his brother. He felt he needed to clarify what he had just said, why he spoke only for himself. They had always been close, never held anything back from each other.

He was sure the menfolk from the church who had come to help, the ones who might possibly have heard what he had said, would understand, but he wanted Jamie to know why none of the rest of the family came with him to meet the train.

Jodie's voice was soft, the expressions on his face keeping pace with what he was telling, as though confident that his brother would be able to hear him, no matter where he was.

"You're probably as aware as I am of all the years that have passed, and I don't reckon I'll ever know about what happened to you, but I do want you to know how things are here, know why I only spoke for myself."

At the sound of one muted owl hoot his features

brightened as he turned warily to his right. It sounded so close, as if Jamie might possibly be right here in the wagon with him.

After a moment the surprise on his face dissolved into a pleasant smile and he turned back to the front. He drew in a breath and let it out slowly before he spoke. "I kinda thought you might be around somewhere, had even hoped you would be, but then I told myself that I was probably expecting way too much."

Jodie rode quietly for a moment, smiling down at the reins he was holding, then looked up as though searching the air around him, looking for something to talk to.

"You know, Jamie. I always wanted to believe that stuff Grandpa Jordan used to tell us. I never really had any reason to doubt anything Grandpa said, but I just couldn't find anything that would let me believe any of that kind of stuff. I couldn't even imagine what a soul was supposed to look like, if I ever saw one."

He rode on quietly for a moment, then spoke softly to himself, like it was an afterthought. "Probably would have scared the bejesus out of me if I had ever come up on anything like that, but it's different with you."

Lester turned in the saddle and looked back at the procession behind him, then drew the reins tighter for a moment to settle his horse down and allow the wagon to catch up. He was as aware as the rest of the people here that Jodie was a loner, and was well aware that he often talked to himself. He was just glad that Jodie had his brother back home again, had someone to talk to if that was what was going on now.

Lester checked on the two men riding the mules. They were keeping up with the wagon and the two men sitting on the tail end, behind the casket, were just riding along, making no effort to eavesdrop, so he turned his attention back to the road as it began to rise ahead of him.

When Jodie felt like he wasn't being watched anymore, he continued. "I want you to know why Momma and Poppa and Rosemary didn't come down here with me to welcome you home." He glanced shyly over to his right for a moment. "I'm all that's left of the family, Jamie."

Grandpa Jordan's stories about souls coming back to watch over their loved ones had begun to come back to him now as he talked. "You probably already know that but I just want to make sure."

He hesitated for a moment, not really sure Jamie knew about Rosemary, then steeled his resolve and continued.

"Rosemary's been gone for a while." He drew in a breath and continued before there was any interference.

"When we was notified that they had lost track of you, that they had declared you Missing-in-Action, Rosemary come over to the house near about every day." He hesitated a moment, then began to shake his head slowly when there was no response, and continued anyway.

"It wasn't more than just a few days before Momma invited Rosemary to stay overnight, told her that she was welcome to use your room instead of driving back and forth all the time, especially in the dark." He hesitated again for a moment before he continued.

"The next morning she just up and left right after breakfast. Momma had been letting her use your truck and she just got up from the breakfast table, went out to your pickup and drove off."

He stopped to think a minute, to be sure and get it right, because from Grandpa Jordan's stories it had just struck him that Jamie might already know.

"But she was back in no more than an hour or so, well before lunch, with some clothes and a few other things to stay the night again."

He shrugged as he hesitated. "Every day or so she brought a few more things until she quit going back home altogether." He shrugged again. "I never did know if it was because Rosemary thought Momma needed consoling or Momma wanted to take care of Rosemary, wanted to help her keep her spirits up."

Jodie looked up and gave the reins a flip to hurry the mules along when he saw Lester's big horse prancing sideways in place again.

"Didn't make no difference which it was, because they got along real good. She helped Momma around the house, helped in the kitchen, done some of the shopping, but I wouldn't let her wash your pickup. I told her that was in my department, that I took care of all the outside work." He smiled sheepishly down at his hands. "I told her that I was the only one here that really knew how you wanted your truck washed."

Jodie couldn't help but smile at the thought of having her there, of having someone to talk to about his brother and do for, the thought of having a sister-in-law.

"Poppa treated her like a daughter-in-law. Treated her like she was already a part of the family. Told her not to worry, that you knew how to take care of yourself, and that one day when the war was over, the train would stop down there at the crossroad and let you off. She smiled and nodded as Poppa told her that Fred would surely give them a blast on the whistle and she could drive down there in your pickup to bring you home. And you know how Poppa always went on about any kind of celebration. Momma would bake a cake and he would butcher a hog."

Jodie smiled at the thought of it. "I was kind of looking forward to something like that myself."

He paused and glanced down at his hands again, tightly holding the reins. He wasn't sure if Poppa had really told her that, but he did remember the two of them setting out on the porch after supper a lot of nights, and Poppa could very well have told her that. He was good at that kind of stuff.

Jodie drew in a sharp breath, as if to fortify himself. "Then one day she come back from shopping, had been gone a lot longer than she usually was, and just put the groceries on the cabinet and went up to her room."
He began to shake his head slowly. "Never did know what happened that day, but she wasn't never the same anymore."

Chapter Forty-Four

Jamie was sorry about what he did that day in the parking lot, sorry it had caused so much trouble, but he would do it again if he had to. He hadn't meant to upset anyone, and certainly not Rosemary, but he had meant to send Orris Fergerson on his way, meant for the man to quit bothering her.

He brought his attention back to his little brother, whose gray hair made him look as if he might have shrunk some, but Jodie's head just kept shaking as he continued.

"Momma and Poppa was beside themselves when she just stayed up there in your room. Oh, she come down at meal times, and still sat on the porch with Poppa after supper some, but he didn't try to question her. Didn't try to find out what had happened. Told Momma that he felt Rosemary would only talk to him about it if it was something he might be able to help her with, or something she especially wanted him to know, but that he really felt the girl would be more likely to confide in her. Would probably be more comfortable talking to Momma."

A soothing warmth engulfed Jamie as he watched his brother. The rascal was always so serious about his family, and Jodie had readily accepted Rosemary as a sister long before he had happily switched her status to that of sister-in-law.

Jodie continued to shake his head as he talked, still letting the mules set their own pace.

"Momma worried over her, tried to get her to talk, talk about anything just so they were talking, then she was so hurt when Rosemary wouldn't. You know, talk, confide in her."

He hesitated for a moment as he struggled with it. "Then when Rosemary started looking a little peaked, started piddling around with her food and losing weight, Momma began to talk to Poppa about it, about what they should do."

Jodie gave the reins a perfunctory flip when he noticed that Lester had stopped in the road again to let them catch up, but the mules were doing okay. They were familiar with this road and had hunkered into their harness when it began to rise before them.

"I tried to talk to her. Tried to cheer her up. Told her about all the plans that you had mentioned to me. About where and what kind of house you wanted to build for her, and the things she wanted that you were going to do. But it just seemed to make things worse."

Jodie hesitated a moment and glanced apologetically over at the seat beside him.

"Then one night while I was sitting on the porch with her, while Poppa was helping Momma with the dishes, and I was going on about what you wanted to do when you got home, she reached over with a little bit of a smile and patted my hand and said she knew. Said that you'uns had already talked about it, said that was what you had told her."

Jamie couldn't get over how his brother had aged, looked like a little old man, but his voice hadn't changed or the obligations he felt towards his family, especially his adopted sister-in-law.

Jodie had leaned forward again with his elbows on his knees, letting the mules continue at their own pace up the hill as he kept talking.

"Momma tried everything she could think of to get Rosemary to eat. Even fixed a breakfast tray a couple of times and took it up to her." Jodie started shaking his head again. "But Rosemary just brought the tray back down to the kitchen when she was dressed."

He glanced over to the seat beside him again as though his brother were bodily sitting there. "Momma said there wasn't enough of it ever gone to feed a sparrow." He turned back toward the front again. "Then Momma started coming at her from the other way around the smoke house. Started telling her that she needed to eat, needed to keep herself in good shape for when you come marching home. Told her how proud you would be to have her standing there beside you for the big wedding."

Jodie sighed as he hesitated again. "But it didn't help. Rosemary just kept drawing away from us, begin to stay up there in her room all the time. Momma and Poppa both worked at taking her meals up there to her, trying to console her, and then one morning Poppa came right back down, still carrying the tray."

Jodie glanced timidly to his right again, hesitating a moment before he spoke, as though weighing what he was going to say. "The only other time I ever remember seeing Poppa cry was when the Army notified us about you, notified us that they had lost track of you."

His voice was low and squeaky as he drew his shirt sleeve across his eyes. "Momma and Poppa just stood there holding each other until Momma drew back, wiping her eyes on her apron, and looked up to ask Poppa what they were going to tell you when you got home."

Jamie was repulsed at the thought of Rosemary grieving that way, of her just wasting away after she realized he was gone, and then him not even being there to greet her. The thought of her floating around out there somewhere, so alone, hopefully trying to find him was frightening.

He wanted to reach out to Jodie, wanted to let his brother know that he would catch up with Rosemary, that he would find her and try to make up for all the anguish and suffering he had caused her. He wanted Jodie to know that he was sorry for all the pain and confusion he had put on them.

Jodie nodded ahead, toward the white steepled church up there on the hill where they were headed. "I told Momma and Poppa that you would want her buried in our family plot and you would be upset if we allowed her to be buried anywhere else."

Jamie was struggling with the fact that she had died, struggling with the fact that she was out there somewhere alone, but hopefully where he could find her.

Jodie gave one big final nod. "So that's what we did. We put her in the shade of that big oak tree at the corner of our plot, and that's where I'm going to put you, Jamie. Right there beside her."

Chapter Forty Five

Things were suddenly moving too fast for Jamie. He felt he had accepted the fact that Rosemary died, and yet the mention of her being in a casket in the ground like that was all wrong. It sounded so cruel even though he realized that it was just her body, her earthly garment, however, the fact of it put her now where he would be able to catch up to her.

It was all so overwhelming. The thought of his body finally being back home and his brother still there to handle things, and fill him in on what had happened over the years. And Rosemary being where he could go to her when he was finished here.

It was all so exciting as he continued to float above the wagon seat, next to his brother who was still talking.

"Some years ago, when one of them guys selling caskets and storm doors came through here, Momma and Poppa took him kinda serious. They didn't buy anything from him but they had the folks over at the Monument Works in town put a real nice tombstone at their burial plot."

Jodie glanced to his right at the wagon seat as though making sure Jamie was paying attention.

"It was some kind of reddish-brown rock with McFarron engraved in big fancy letters across the top. Not so fancy that you couldn't read it, but nice, like some of the other monuments in the cemetery. They had Momma's name and birth year put on the left side and Poppa's name and birth year put on the right side."

Jodie paused as he checked on Lester up ahead, then the casket behind him to make sure it was riding okay, the two men on the back of the wagon and the two on the mules following along behind. When he decided everything was in order he brought his gaze back to the seat beside him. His attention stayed on the wagon seat a moment longer than it did on the other points of interest, then smiled at the thought of having his brother back to talk to, and continued.

"So after Rosemary slipped away from us and we got permission from her folks to bury her in our plot, I tried to talk to Momma and Poppa about a nice stone for her," then quickly added, "and you when your time come."

He timidly glanced to his right again. "They liked the idea but was still so broke up that they just nodded and told me do whatever I felt you would want us to do."

Jodie paused as they approached the first turn in the zigzagging road up the mountain, making sure the mules didn't cut the corner too short and crimp the front wheels or upset the wagon, then settled back into the seat and continued.

"So I went over to the Monument Works to talk to Mr. Modglin about a tombstone like the one he had put in for Momma and Poppa." Jodie glanced quickly to his right again.

"When I told him I wanted a tombstone for Rosemary

he nodded and smiled so nice, but then when I told him I wanted one just like the one he had put in for Momma and Poppa, and I wanted the McFarron name on it, the smile disappeared. He just stood there giving me that beady eyed stare, you know, how he looks at anybody who has dared to expect him to step outside the boundaries of his toleration for anything."

Jodie chuckled softly to himself without looking up. "But I didn't let it stop me from telling him that I wanted Rosemary's name on the left side with her birth and death years, and your name on the right side with your birth year, and a blank place for when your time come."

Jodie chuckled softly again at the thought of it. "Mr. Modglin stepped back and looked down at me like he looked down at little Bud that time the boy wet himself in church, you remember, it was during the sermon while he was holding the boy on his lap."

Jodie kept his eyes straight ahead as though Jamie might think he wasn't being serious enough; think he was being disrespectful of Mr. Modglin. When nothing happened, there was no sign of any kind, Jodie let his breath out slowly and continued. "He told me to go have a seat on the bench out front while he called Poppa."

He gave the reins a flick as he worked at keeping a straight face, not wanting to appear smug while he continued. "When I got home I could tell that Poppa was a little more than just peeved, and since there wasn't nothing else going on, it was probably about the phone call."

"After supper that night, when Poppa had cooled down some, and me and him and Momma were setting on the front porch he said that he had told Arthur, I had never heard Mr. Modglin's first name before, that the State does not require a permit or license or any kind of official written approval to bury sweethearts side by side, under one name, in the same burial plot as long as they are in separate caskets, and both caskets are locked."

Jodie glanced timidly over at the wagon seat, almost sure that Jamie wouldn't be offended by the levity, then added Momma's silent assent in case Jamie might feel that Poppa had been too hasty. "Momma leaned around me to make sure Poppa saw her sternly nod her second to what he had told Mr. Modglin."

Jamie was so happy to be back home, and listening to his little brother, even if he really wasn't there and never would be again. He was so thankful, and not really surprised at the way his family had accepted Rosemary and took care of her for him.

He suddenly realized that Jodie had started talking again, in an even more somber tone.

"It wasn't long after that when Momma started having a bad day every once and again but we just laid it to losing Rosemary. Me and Poppa tried to help her keep her mind off all the things that had happened, but she just seemed to not care anymore. Oh, she took care of things like she always did, cooking and cleaning, taking care of the house, but she never talked much anymore."

Jodie leaned forward with his elbows on his knees, the reins held loosely in his hands, talking softly, as if he had rehearsed what he wanted to tell his brother when he got home.

Talking to his brother this way was not exactly what he had hoped for, but it was okay. It would have been much easier and much more enjoyable if they were sitting on the big front porch with a pitcher of lemonade or iced tea, but Jamie needed to know before he went on to wherever it is you go for your next life. Grandpa Jordan had never went that far into it.

Between Grandpa Jordan's stories, Sunday School, Vacation Bible School and Poppa, Jodie was pretty sure of what he was doing now. Pretty sure that his brother was where he could hear him and sure that a soul goes on to their next life when their reason for hanging around here on Earth had been completed.

Chapter Forty-Six

Jodie quietly leaned forward in the seat, holding the reins, just watching the mules as they kept their ears laid back, hunkering farther into their harness as the road continued to rise before them. He couldn't even imagine what Jamie had gone through, what he had to do to get his body back this far, but he wanted his brother to know everything that had happened here. He wanted him to know where everybody was and that his efforts in getting his body back home was appreciated.

Jodie wanted his brother to know that he, with the help of the men from the church, would complete what was left to be done here, and Jamie would be free to go on and catch up with Rosemary, and Momma and Poppa and whatever came next.

Jamie could sense the struggle his little brother was having, the rascal had always been so concerned that things were done right, but there was no way he could think of to help him, nothing more he could do now.

Jodie finally dipped his head and continued. "Then

when Momma left us, Poppa took it pretty well, said Momma was in a better place now, where she could look after Rosemary until we found you."

He drew in a breath and wiped his sleeve across his eyes again. Me and Poppa put Momma up there in her place at the tombstone, had Mr. Modglin put her death year on it, then just went on, taking care of each other while we waited for you."

Jamie regretted that he hadn't been there to greet Momma either, but he was sure Momma and Rosemary both would understand when they were all back together again.

Jodie continued, talking quietly to his brother. "Then Poppa began to change, wouldn't shave of a morning once in a while, would wear the same clothes more than a day or two, and started poking at his food. I laid it to my cooking, but then Mrs. Burgess from the church, who came in a day or two a week to help with the house and laundry, started cooking all kinds of good stuff while she was here working around the house."

He began to shake his head slowly. "But even that didn't help. I knew he missed Momma a lot. I could hear him talking to her out on the porch at night while I washed the supper dishes and cleaned up the kitchen. He would tell her to take good care of Rosemary and he would be on along after you got home and could help me take care of the place here."

He shrugged, still shaking his head quietly. "But, anyway, Poppa didn't make it, gave up too soon. He had been gone a few years when I got the letter from the Army that they had found your body and what they would do with it unless the family had other wishes."

"The letter was addressed to Poppa and Momma but I answered it and explained who I was, the only family member left, and what I wanted them to do with your body. I told them to just send it home and I would take care of it."

He rolled his eyes around to glance at the wagon seat without being too conspicuous. "It was several weeks before I got another letter telling me that they would do that. The letter was in a heavier envelope and I could tell there was something in there besides the letter."

He turned in the seat now to look beside him. "When I opened the envelope and shook it a pretty gold bracelet fell out. It was sealed in a clear plastic packet, and I could see that yours and Rosemary's names were engraved on it. The letter said it had been in the pocket of your uniform, the only personal effects on your body when it was found."

Jodie glanced back and forth between the road ahead and the seat, as though waiting for an answer of some kind for a moment before he continued. "There was no information on where or when you died, or even how. I felt that as long as it has been since they lost you there was no way of knowing or they would have put it in their letter."

He paused and glanced up, trying to think if he had left anything out. Lester's horse was still prancing in spite of the steepness of the road, and the mules were earning their rations, as Grandpa Jordan used to say.

"I took the bracelet with me when I went over to the Monument Works to talk to Bud Modglin about finishing the tombstone. He has been taking care of the place since Mr. Modglin went on to his reward."

"Mrs. Modglin actually runs the place, does the paperwork and stuff like that, and Bud does the sweat work. They had already sent him to school to learn how to work with stone before Mr. Modglin died."

Jodie shifted in the seat and grabbed his knee to move his bad foot to another position, then checked around him and continued. "I had already gone over there and told Bud and his mother that your body had been found and was on its way home and that I didn't have the year of your death."

He kept his eyes straight ahead, like he was ashamed of the fact that he was not going to be able to complete the job like he wanted to. Like he wanted everything to be perfect for the arrival of his brother's body.

"Mrs. Modglin said there had been times in the past that this had happened and they had just put the word 'unknown' in place of the year, but then said that she had read in one of their tombstone books that a lot of places, when the death year wasn't known, especially in military cemeteries, that they just put the letters 'KBTG'. Known But To God."

Jodie hesitated, not sure if he was waiting for some kind of a sign that it would be okay. "I thought about having them just leave the space blank in case the Army come up with more information later on, surely the year, and then I showed them the bracelet."

"Mrs. Modglin wanted to know all about it but I could only tell her that you had either not had a chance to mail it or you was waiting to give it to Rosemary when you was home on your next leave."

He glanced at the seat before he continued. "She said that while Bud was cutting the letters in the stone he could cut a slot in the top, insert the   bracelet and reseal it. She said that way it would be there with the two of you from now on."

Jodie chuckled quietly to himself at the thought of Bud working on the tombstone there in the cemetery. Bud was skeptical of Grandpa's stories about souls hanging around, but he could possibly feel now that both Jamie and Rosemary would be there watching him hide the bracelet.

Then a smile crossed Jodie's face. Probably Momma and Poppa and Grandma and Grandpa, too.

"So I told them to go ahead." And he had hoped that nothing would happen to give Bud the idea that the whole family was there watching.

Chapter Forty-Seven

Jodie looked up to see that Lester had reached the gravelled parking lot that lay in front and around to the side of the church, and was waiting in the shade of one of the large trees surrounding it. His horse blowed a couple of times, tossing its head up and down at the smell of the water in the mossy trough at the well beside the church.

Jodie was still trying to put it together in his mind to gently tell Jamie that they were going to have a little bit of a ceremony before they buried his body next to Rosemary's back there in the cemetery tomorrow.

As the mules approached the shaded church lot he drew in a long breath and glanced toward the seat beside him.

"I told the Army people that you would just want to be brought home and buried in the family plot. I told our pastor the same thing, as well as the war veterans that are members of our church. They all came by the house when they found out your body was on its way home."

"The pastor is new, Jamie. Hasn't been here much

over a year yet, and I didn't know he was a veteran, too, or had been a chaplain. All the veterans refer to him as 'Padre', and he, along with all of them insisted that you most surely had earned the honor of a military funeral."

Jodie turned his attention back to the mules, and continued. "I told the preacher that I was following your wishes as well as I knew, so I finally agreed to an all night visitation, with our local veterans here standing Honor Guard throughout the night. I understand there are enough volunteers for them to stand two hour shifts through the end of the funeral tomorrow. He said their wives and daughters would come in to keep the coffee pots going, fix some sandwiches and cinnamon rolls, and have a hot breakfast ready for everybody in the morning."

He carefully turned the mules into the lot, then alongside the church and stopped with the back of the wagon even with the front of the building. He wasn't going to attempt to back up to the door when there were enough men here to carry the casket from the wagon into the church. They could place it on the stand they and the pastor had constructed last week and covered with a green skirt. They called it a cataflaque. It would remain there through the night, until the ceremony tomorrow morning.

While the two men from the back of the wagon got down, and the other two hitched their mules to the hitching posts at the edge of the parking lot, Jodie climbed slowly down from the seat of the wagon.

He struggled with the two iron weights under the seat, taking them down one at a time and placing one in front of each mule. He bent down at each mule to ground hitch the animal, then laboriously made his way along the wagon bed and heaved himself backwards onto the edge that the two men had just vacated, and scooted back to lean against the casket.

Jamie watched his brother draw his shirt sleeve across his forehead, then just sit there as if waiting for Jamie to drift in and hover next to him.

His little brother had always been so concerned with 'pulling his own freight', as he put it, even though he was slower now. Jamie was beginning to realize that his brother wasn't so young anymore, but apparently still concerned with not being considered a burden because of his foot.

Jodie turned unconsciously to look up at the little whisp of vapor hanging over the end of the casket as if he might see his brother in what he saw as just a reflection from somewhere.

"In the morning our pastor will conduct a short ceremony in the church. A burial team from one of the veterans service organizations in town will come out to handle the military part of it, then escort the casket to the grave back there beside Rosemary."

He wiped his eyes and his forehead with his shirt sleeve again and settled back to look down at his hands. "The pastor said the burial team would conduct their own military service at the grave, but I balked when he said that would include a twenty-one gun salute."

He glanced toward the wagon bed beside him, shaking his head sternly. "I don't think there will be that much of a crowd back there in the morning, but we don't need a bunch of city boys out here waving their guns around, even if they are firing into the air."

Jamie felt that cradling warmth again. That was pure Jodie, so concerned, so careful to do what was right in his own mind.

Jodie hadn't looked up. "Then the pastor explained that there would only be seven of them and the team would fire three separate volleys, using blank ammunition, and then a bugler somewhere closeby, but out of sight, would play taps."

He turned again as if he were looking at his brother, and began to nod while he drew his shirt sleeve across his eyes again. "That's when I told them to go ahead with it, Jamie."

The glowing warmth held Jamie as he watched his brother take out his handkerchief and blow his nose and return it to his pocket, then draw his sleeve across his eyes again.

"When our high school class went to Washington, D.C., for our senior trip, that was after you had been drafted, I heard that played at the Tomb of the Unknown Soldier."

He wiped his eyes again with the heels of his hands as he talked, still looking at the wagon bed beside him, settling himself more comfortably against the casket.

"I can still hear it, Jamie. All they've been giving us about you through the years is unknown, unknown, so I felt you deserved it as much as whoever they got buried in that tomb up there. I thought it was so reverent, almost like praying, that I told our pastor to go ahead. Told him that I wanted you to have it, too."

Jodie sat quietly for a moment, looking down as he wiped his hands on his pants, then just his eyebrows raised as he started talking again, just above a whisper. "I never gave up on you, Jamie. I knew you would come back to us however you could. Momma never gave up hope, either. When she began to fail, Momma said the Good Lord would watch over you, and if not before, we'd all meet again in Heaven someday."

He drew his shirt sleeve across his eyes again. "I'm so thankful that Momma was right, and The Man up there helped you bring your body home. I'm just sorry that Momma and Poppa are gone, and Rosemary." He paused and started shaking his head slowly. "We never knew what happened to her that day she come back from grocery shopping, but we done the best we could.

He scooted to the edge of the wagon bed and lowered himself to the ground, then just stood there watching Lester slide his long rifle back into its scabbard and dismount.

His voice was still low as he talked, as if he were oblivious to what was going on around him. "That girl loves you, Jamie. She used to talk about when you got back home, about all the things you'uns were going to do, but after that day she come back from shopping, she quit talking, quit doing just about everything else, too."

Jodie turned to face the casket, moving his hands over the folds as though checking to make sure the flag was still in place.

"You've done your part in getting your body back home, so you need to go on now and check in with Momma and Poppa, and Rosemary. They're waiting up there for you, Jamie. I'll take care of things here."

He reached up as though brushing dust from the flag. "You remember what Grandpa used to tell us about departed souls watching their own funeral, about them being there hoping to console their loved ones. I can see you now, sitting up there with Rosemary, and Momma and Poppa, tomorrow morning while that guy blows taps." He paused and looked up as an impish smile crossed his face.

One low owl hoot had seemed to rise from the casket, then as Lester turned and headed his way, there was another one off in the distance. "You go on now, Jamie. And if something ain't done exactly right here, just give me a two hooter and I'll take care of it."

He drew his shirt sleeve across his eyes and turned as Lester approached. "Sure wish we could get some rain, need to cut down on all that road dust."

"Yeah, I know." Lester gave his shoulders one more slap with his hat before he replaced it on his head. "Caught a little of it myself, and I was riding way out there in front."

Chapter Forty-Eight

Jamie slowed and hovered about halfway between the scene of the activity at the church and the dim glow that had stayed on the horizon all this time. He had begun to give some thought to going to the light when he finally got his body on the way home, but he hadn't dwelled too much on what it would actually be like beyond the light. Particularly what would be forgiven and what would be accountable.

His failure at being a soldier still bothered him. There was his grandparents, the only family that he expected to be there to greet him. He wasn't afraid to face them, not Grandpa Jordan and Grandma Olga, but they might not recognize him after all this time, or they could have possibly gone on to wherever you go next.

He was a little vague on how souls would recognize each other without their bodies, anyway, and he so wanted to believe that his failure as a soldier wouldn't really matter to Grandpa and Grandma. He wanted to believe that an earthly failing would not extend beyond the light.

He had realized long ago that he couldn't go back home again, could only see that his body got there to let them know he wasn't a deserter. Let them know why he hadn't come back home when the war was over.

The short contact he had just had with Jodie had stirred him to want to stay there with his little brother, to actually want to return home to a life like it had been before he had been drafted. The two of them could sit on the porch and talk about all the things that had happened. He was sure that Jodie would have no trouble in bringing him up to date on everything that had happened since he was drafted.

But now he realized that with Momma and Poppa and Rosemary gone, it wouldn't be the same. Time Marches On, as Grandpa Jordan used to say, but all that ever meant to him and Jodie back then was how quick they had to go back to school in the fall.

Jamie stayed where he was and turned to see the church. He watched the men gather around the wagon with Lester at the back and two of the other men on each side as they lifted the casket and moved away   from the wagon. Jodie had opened the front doors of the church and now stood aside as they came up the steps.

When Lester stepped up the one step into the entrance vestibule he turned to walk backwards and removed his hat, then turned again, walking sideways while he guided the procession into the church.

Each of the other men also removed their hats before they stepped into the vestibule. They each struggled one-handedly with the casket as they moved solemnly down the aisle, the hand holding their hat waving in rhythm with each laden stride.

They approached the waiting cataflague in front of the altar and stopped. Lester positioned the stand, then knelt down to guide them in placing the flag draped casket squarely on it.

Jamie watched his brother follow them into the church, then turn and move along the back wall to the other aisle on the right. Jodie grabbed onto the end of each pew, pulling himself along as he made his way up to where the Pastor waited. They both stood ready to help the men settle the casket onto the improvised cataflague.

The sensation of warmth engulfed Jamie again as he hesitated for a moment, watching his brother's concern for his body. When the casket was finally in place Jamie turned and moved slowly toward the light that seemed to become less formidable the closer he got.

And his apprehension became less severe the closer he got to the light and its soft glow. The calming sensation continued, despite his feelings of a superior being beyond its scope, and it wasn't due to Momma and Poppa already being there.

He was almost sure they would forgive him, even if they knew, but he had never been led to believe that folks up here sat around and discussed their life on earth or talked about how they died. And even if they did, Momma and Poppa had passed on before Jodie had heard from the Army.

But he wasn't sure about how to approach Rosemary. She didn't know how he died, but she did realize that day in the parking lot that he was gone. He had caused her so much trouble and heartache that he would probably never live.., he stopped at the word, he wasn't sure how time was measured up there beyond the light, but however it was handled it would take a long time for him to make it up to her.

A slight chill threatened the warmth he had been sensing. Even if she still cared for him, was waiting for him up here, he would have to find her, and find a way to make it up to her. Would have to find a way to show her how much he cared, show her how much he still loved her.

He thought again of her sitting there in the parking lot in his truck that day after he had scared Orris Fergersen away. He had wanted so badly to put his arm around her and comfort her, wanted to tell her everything would be alright, but he couldn't be sure it wouldn't just frighten her further. And besides, he didn't have an arm anymore, didn't know of any way to reach her even if he did.

Jamie reluctantly glanced back at the activity in the church, then turned slowly toward the light again. He had never really considered what would actually take place after he got his body home, got it in the hands of his family, and finally went on to the light.

He guessed he had just taken it for granted that he would be there with Grandpa and Grandma, and would have no problem with greeting each member of his family as their turn came to arrive. He had been sure that he could handle greeting Momma and Poppa and Jodie as they arrived up here one at a time, and reasonably sure that he could handle the arrival of Rosemary, even though he had caused her so much heartache.

A brief coolness floated across his confidence at the thought of all of them except Jodie already being there.

The eerie feeling stayed with him as the native village came into view, and the original Chief who had rescued his body from the jungle. The Chief's funeral, with its ceremonial bonfires, ritual dancing and chanting, reminded him that the man was already up here, too.

Then as the blazing fires began to fade, the scene changed to the bleak countryside and the drab barracks and buildings of the salt mine. He had seen GA there, but not Rebel, and that had worried him.

Their bodies may never be found, but there was

nothing their guards could do to keep their souls from arriving up here. He wouldn't doubt that Rebel was already here and from the haggard condition of GA, if he wasn't here yet it probably wouldn't be much longer.

Jamie wasn't sorry that he had made sure his body was found and returned home, but he needed to let the old Chief know how he felt. Let the man know that he would be forever grateful to him and the entire village for their concern and all their kindnesses.

As Jamie drifted closer to the light his thoughts of the Chief, the village and its people, and the bleak countryside where his two friends were, began to fade and a different kind of warmth, a more personal and much deeper sensation moved in to possess him.

The sudden thrill of another presence and the elation of its air of familiarity was startling.

A slowly turning column of vapor hesitated for just a moment between him and the light, then swirled out and engulfed him. He caught a faint whiff of the perfume he had given Rosemary, then he felt the sensation of her gentle breath. Like he used to feel on his neck when they no longer needed to talk and just snuggled together.

An intense exhilaration swept over Jamie as they moved closer to the light and entered its soft glow.